THE JESTER

The Fae Court
Book 1

ALEXIS BROOKE

ARCANE PASSION PRESS

Arcane Passion Press is an imprint of A.P Beswick Publications Ltd.

ISBN:

Hardback - 978-1-916671-29-4

Paperback - 978-1-916671-28-7

Editing - Quinn Nichols, Quill And Bone Editing

Cover Design by Krafigs Design

Remember that sometimes it's the villain who needs a safe word....

Trigger Warnings

This book includes but not limited to the following triggers.

Graphic Sexual Content
Flogging
Rope Play
Injury And Death

THE JESTER

Chapter One

ALANA

I slide the gilded mask onto my face and fasten it behind my ears. Tonight, I will go unnoticed. I won't be the girl who did the unspeakable thing. I won't be stared at. Men will not shy away from my touch.

I will dance, and flirt, and laugh, and no one will be afraid of me because they will not know who I am. My costume – and its magic – will make sure of that.

There is a tap on the door, prompting me to quickly pull the mask off and slip it back into the trunk at the foot of my bed.

"Please enter," I reply, picking up a book and positioning myself by the window as though this is where I intend to stay for the remainder of the evening.

Rawk enters with a stride that sharply slaps the wooden boards. "Alana." He folds his arms. His wings are out, deep purple, still as the ocean before a storm.

Mine twitch with unease; they have a habit of betraying my emotions and, unlike the rest of my body, I have still not learned to tame them.

I put down the book and close the gap between us.

Rawk is older than me by one hundred years. He is one of the older fae in the village, and is anticipating being named an elder when he reaches his next half-century. He is not old enough to carry the amount of ego that swells in his overly large biceps. But he is old enough to be trusted to *contain* me this evening.

He quirks an eyebrow, clearly expecting me to speak. When I don't, he clicks his fingers and I hold out my forearms.

"Where are your gloves?" he asks, his jaw ticking with irritation.

I motion to the dresser where my purple elbow-length gloves are draped neatly over the mirror. "I wasn't expecting visitors."

With a hesitant but swift movement, Rawk swipes the gloves from the mirror and holds them in front of me. "Put them on," he says roughly.

I do as he asks, slipping into their familiar embrace with a sigh.

Rawk nods, then takes a set of silver cuffs from his waist-band and secures them on my wrists. On top of the gloves.

"The cuffs are just for tonight, Alana. You understand why," he says, his gaze catching on mine. He smiles. But it was not sympathy that prompted his remark. It was the hope that I would *read* it as sympathy and finally agree to fuck him.

And *that* is the great irony of my situation; although they are scared of me, every male in my village wants to be the one to tame me. The one to control my magic. The one who fucks Alana the Untouchable and escapes unharmed. With his mind intact.

I would not allow Rawk between my legs if he was the last fae in the kingdom. And if I did, I would certainly not leave him intact.

"Just for tonight," I reply sweetly.

He stands for a moment, his wings still unnervingly still. Then he looks me up and down, makes a tutting sound in the back of his throat, and pulls the door roughly shut on his way out.

"May the moon be in your favour," I call after him – as is custom on the night of the Forest Moon centennial.

Clearly, Rawk does not see me as worthy of receiving custom.

I move to the window then, tilting my head from side to side, I let down the gates that keep my mind from feeling those around me. It took me too long to master this skill. Far too long. Other empaths can do it from the day they are born, but not me.

My mother used to say I struggled because I was so much stronger than those who'd come before me. My father believed the opposite.

My kin – the other Leafborne fae of the forest – sided with

my father. They hated me long before I gave them reason to.

Allowing the sounds, and movements, and emotions of the forest to swell inside my skull, I press my forehead to the glass and search for Rawk. He is no longer close by. My cabin, on the outskirts of the village, is surrounded by silence.

I can feel the others in the distance – their excitement, the hedonistic murmur of their hearts as they put on their costumes and drink their wine. But they are muted. Far enough away that I am confident I am alone.

I look down at my wrists. The cuffs are designed to prevent me from changing as the others will. For tonight, the night of the Forest Moon, is the night my people become one with the world around them.

On this one night – just one – every century, the Leafborne fae of the outermost forests are able to change form and be true kin with the creatures of the land.

At the last Forest Moon festival, Kayan, Rosalie, and I spent the evening as owls. We flew high into the treetops and watched everything that was happening down below. We watched the deer rutting and tried to figure out who they were, and whether they'd be horrified or delighted when they shifted back and realised who they'd just fucked. We hunted, we soared, and then we returned to the fire at sunrise and gathered with the others for the breaking dawn ceremony.

It was the best night of my life.

And the day after became the worst.

I run my fingers over the silver cuffs. They are tight, but not linked, so I can still move freely. I let a deep breath swell in the crevices between my ribs, then exhale slowly and retrieve my mask from its hiding place.

Swiftly, I slide it back on, then tug my purple gloves free from beneath the cuffs and replace them with the gold ones from the bottom of my trunk. I sigh as I look at the gold fabric. At first, the deep-purple gloves my mother gave me meant freedom. Freedom from absorbing others' emotions at the slightest brush of the hand.

But in the one hundred years since the last Forest Moon, they have become nothing more than symbols of my failings. Failure to control. Failure to free myself.

I move to the wardrobe, reach inside, and loosen the hidden panel at the back. Then I take out my dress. The dress I've spent the last century building just for tonight.

Retracting my wings, I remove my emerald-green gown, allow it to pool at my feet, then step out of it and slip on my costume. It feels like feathers of silk against my skin. I release my wings once more, and flex them gently into a satisfying stretch.

In front of the dressing table, I assess my reflection.

For now, I still look like me. Fiery auburn hair hanging in waves over my shoulders. A slender silhouette. Pale skin.

Against my hair, the mask glistens, emphasising my porcelain complexion but hiding the splash of freckles across my nose. It is intricately carved, and makes my sea-green eyes dazzle when they catch the dimming evening light. It was my mother's, but now it is mine. And the weight of the enchantments that are laced into its fibres rest heavily on my brow.

I adjust the mask, then smooth my hands over my dress, skimming my sides and my hips.

This dress – oh, this dress! The hours I have spent weaving incantations into the silk threads, poring over books from my mother's library, searching for magics that have long been forgotten by the Leafborne who walk the forests today.

All so I can go to the centennial and walk amongst my kin without being seen.

In this dress, my magic will keep them from seeing me as I am. They will see an illusion – whoever they *want* to see. Someone who makes them feel safe and at ease. Someone who makes them smile. If they speak to me, they will hear the voice of that person. If they dance with me, they will feel the body of that person. And as soon as I leave their sight, they will forget it ever happened.

I have tested it once.

On Rosalie.

Although she speaks to me more than the others, it had been a long time since we were alone and it was both wonderful and heartbreaking at the same time.

But it worked.

She didn't see me; she saw her cousin. We talked about the weather, and the new herd of white horses that had moved into the valley beyond the falls. Then she told me she'd see me at dinner that evening, and walked away.

Dragging my thoughts away from my friend, I apply some red colouring to my lips, then brush my hair one final time.

My mother would love this dress.

Its whisper-thin silk will shift from the deepest midnight blue to a deep, hypnotic purple, depending on how the moonlight kisses the fabric. The hem has been enchanted to flutter gently, as if caught in a perpetual, soft breeze. And around my waist, I wear a belt of woven silver vines that accentuates my waist and my hips.

Everything about this dress has been designed to dazzle those who see it. In this dress, I will walk among the other fae of my village completely free of judgement because they will not see me.

The mask and the enchantments will hide me from them. From those who remember what I did.

As the memory snags on the deepest crevices of my mind, my stomach constricts and my excitement darkens.

What if there isn't *enough* magic to enchant again and again and again for an entire evening? What if I am exposed, and exiled for my betrayal?

For a fraction of a moment, I consider taking off the dress and the mask and staying here.

But I know I will not.

I cannot.

I cannot remain on the outskirts of my own life for much longer without losing my mind.

I wait until the sun dips beyond the umbrella of the forest's canopy before leaving my cabin. Barefoot, I nestle my toes into the dark green moss that carpets the floor. I stand for a moment, allowing beads of evening dew to cool my soles.

I adjust my mask, my dress, my gloves.

Then I walk towards the noise of the celebration.

As I weave through the most dense part of the forest, twilight clings to the trees, the last fading rays of dusk filtering through the canopy in slanted beams. When I reach the stream, violet butterflies spiral upwards at my feet, their delicate wings casting flickering shadows across the twisted roots and rocks by the river's edge.

With each stride, excitement sparks brighter within me, fizzing hotter and stronger than the apprehension that grips my chest.

Closer to the clearing, the trees begin to thin. Towering oaks and firs creak softly in the gentle breeze. Gnarled and covered in velvet green moss, they watch my passage and sigh at me.

"Everything will be okay," I whisper. More to myself than to them.

Pausing, I trail my fingers along the bark of my favourite tree, feeling the thrum of life pulsing in its core. Unlike the cold, unfeeling stone of the kingdom's cities, everything here is *alive*.

I visited Luminael – our capital – only once, and vowed never to go there again. Perhaps that is why I didn't flee when I should have – why I stayed and allowed myself to become a shadow in my own life.

Finally, the clearing comes into view. I inhale deeply, letting the air feed my lungs. For a long moment, I soak up the swirling tendrils of revelry and joy that float in the air. I let the excitement and the anticipation wash over me.

I'm about to slam the gates back down and spend the evening revelling in only my own thoughts, when something stops me.

On this night when everyone is happy, and when no one will look at me and feel fear, why not fill myself with joy and light instead of darkness?

So, leaving my gates down, I emerge into the clearing.

It has been an entire century since the last Forest Moon, and the things that happened after have since erased any positive memories from my mind.

But now, they come flooding back.

Familiarity and hedonistic exhilaration flood my senses.

A bonfire blazes in the centre of the clearing, flames licking up towards the starry sky as fae dancers whirl around the fire in a mesmerising blur of colour and movement. Sparks of magic crackle through the air, taking shape as birds and butterflies and ethereal shapes with no solid form.

Tonight, everyone is masked and everyone wears an elaborate costume.

I wait for heads to turn, but no one notices my arrival. Relief washes over me, the weight of one hundred years finally slipping from my shoulders. My wings unfurl, tingling with the promise of unbridled freedom. Finally, I am not a monster.

For this one night, I am not a monster.

I am not myself.

I am free.

But then I see him.

Chapter Two

ALANA

I'd know him anywhere. Broad shoulders, curly blond hair. He turns slightly and I catch sight of his wings. When we knew each other – when he loved me – they had blue tips and veins of silver like the other Leafborne fae whose magic can compel the element of water.

Now, they are pale. Grey and paper thin; more like a Shadowkind fae than a Leafborne. I can see the firelight through them as he moves.

I flex my fingers inside my gold gloves. Even though I know they will protect him from me, fear drips like ice water through my veins. What if I get too close?

In my head, I rehearse what I will say. "Evening Kayan . . . Hey, Kayan. Hi, Kayan, how are you?"

"Beautiful dress. Let me guess. Tonight, you will be changing into a peacock. Blues, purples, and golds. Strutting through the forest like a queen."

A voice with a timbre like warm honey pulls my gaze away from Kayan.

It is a voice I do not recognise, and I instinctively take a step back. The owner of the voice smiles at me from beneath a deep blood-red mask. It covers his entire face. Everything except his eyes, which are so dark they look like nothing more than pools of ink amidst the blood.

Taller than me, the stranger moves to block my line of sight – as if he knows I am staring at Kayan and wants to distract me from him.

"A peacock? Is that what you think of me? A preening, strutting, princess?" I ask, folding my arms as my wings twitch with annoyance. But as I stare at him, the annoyance fades. Because it is not arrogance emanating in waves from his athletic frame – it is *wanting*.

He wants me.

Not in the way Rawk wants me.

He wants me in a way that is both pure and powerfully disarming at the same time.

It has been so long since I felt this way – and the strength of his lust is so sudden – I almost forget how to breathe.

As a glimmer of the person I once was stirs in my belly, I move closer to him and tilt my head, leaning into the sensation I'm starting to remember. "We have not even had a conversation, and already you are insulting me? Does that usually work for you?" A coy smile twitches on my lips.

The stranger's eyes twinkle. Although I cannot see his lips, I know he is smiling because the air around him shimmers with pleasure as I speak.

He releases a low chuckle that sends a small hum of enjoyment to colour my cheeks. "I'd have to spend more time with you in order to answer that question," he says, extending his hand to take mine.

I hesitate, then hold my breath in my chest and accept the gesture. Instead of shaking my hand, he kisses it, meeting my eyes as his mask brushes the fabric of my gloves. Despite the fact our skin is not touching, something inside me fizzes as I watch him looking up at me.

"May I ask your name?" He straightens, clasping his hands together behind his back as though he is a suitor and I am a princess.

I open my mouth to reply, but my voice snags in my throat. He should know my name, or at least he should *think* he knows my name. If the spell is working, I should appear to him as someone familiar. Someone he already knows.

Panic stiffens in my bones. If this stranger sees me for who I really am, perhaps the enchantments aren't working. Perhaps I am about to be found out . . .

Except that cannot be so, because if the enchantments had dropped, I would have been noticed immediately and would already be on my way to exile in the shadowlands.

"Varia." I take my mother's name and try not to mind that the lie tastes like acid on my tongue. Why does it feel wrong to lie to this man? Why do I feel as though he already knows me even though the opposite is quite clearly true?

"It's a pleasure to meet you, Varia."

"And you?" I wait for him to give me *his* name but he does

not. Instead he winks at me – *winks* at me – and saunters away in the direction of the bonfire.

"I will seek your company later," he calls. "When the dancing begins."

A little stunned, I tuck my hair behind my ear and exhale slowly. The juxtaposition of feeling suddenly *seen* and being reminded of the very reason I have been invisible for so long is hard to process.

Staring at Kayan does not help.

I'm about to draw myself away, follow the stream to the waterfall where the first dance will be starting, when he looks in my direction.

My breath falters, and a hand goes involuntarily to my stomach. Kayan smiles. He raises an arm and waves at me. I have no idea who he sees me as, but I wave back.

I am completely frozen. I cannot move. I search for the stranger who called me a peacock because perhaps he is nearby and will spot that I am uneasy. But he has disappeared.

"Rosalie . . ." Kayan puts a firm hand on my shoulder, then kisses my neck. The place just below my ear. A wave of contentment washes over me. But it is not my emotion; it is his.

My heart strains against the confines of my ribcage, and I swallow a knot of irony that tastes metallic in my mouth. They are together? He and Rosalie are together?

As he draws away from me, I can still feel the burn of his kiss. Like a tattoo on my skin, I fear it will remain there forever. "Kayan." I smile and tuck myself into his embrace.

A firm hand runs down my back. Oh, how I remember his hands. "I wish I could change with you tonight," he whispers, his forehead coming to rest against mine.

My body has stiffened beneath his touch. Memories are clawing to be noticed, but I do my best to ignore them and force myself to stroke his forearm in return. "I'll be thinking of you." I step back and look into his eyes.

For the first time in one hundred years, I stare into his beautiful eyes. But they are not the same as they were. The magic is gone. "I'm sorry," I say quietly.

He frowns and tucks his index finger beneath my chin. "What do you have to be sorry for?"

There are so many things I want to say – things I was never allowed to say because he couldn't bring himself to be anywhere near me after I broke him. But that would be selfish. So, instead, I shake my head, laugh, and say, "I'm sorry tonight is hard for you."

Kayan's smile falters. "I'm fine," he says, a little stiffly.

"You're strong." I slip my hand into his.

He looks down, and I wonder whether he is seeing a version of Rosalie who wears golden gloves or if he sees her hands – long, lithe fingers, turquoise and gold rings, soft palms.

"You have survived so much." I keep his gaze for as long as I can before forcing myself to look away. Over my shoulder, I pretend I have seen someone I need to speak to, then stroke his cheek one last time, tell him I will find him later, and hurry into the shadows beyond the bonfire.

From here, I watch, tears rolling down my cheeks and slicking the inside of my mask.

The rules of the enchantment are that the recipient of the spell should forget they have seen me – or the person they *thought* I was – as soon as I am out of sight. So, when the real Rosalie comes into view, skipping over to Kayan with her broad smile and her bouncy blond hair, he greets her as if for the first time.

Everything is working as I intended it to. He embraces her the way he embraced me a moment ago. He kisses her neck the way he kissed mine. Except, the real Rosalie does not react to him the way I did. She giggles, lightheartedly punches him on the arm, then flits into the air and circles him, flirting with every fibre of her slim blond body.

Kayan's jaw twitches and he swallows forcefully. He cannot fly anymore. And, although I'm sure she means it in fun, to an outsider it looks almost as if she is taunting him with this knowledge.

Rosalie never did think about things the way I did; could never anticipate others' emotions the way I can.

Eventually, as they start to embrace, I tear myself away, return to the stream, and follow it in the direction of the waterfall.

I have no idea why tonight, of all nights, it is this place I am drawn to. It holds so many memories that – for an entire century – I have avoided it. And yet, it is as beautiful now as it was then.

Shimmering in the moonlight, the pool is crystal clear, disturbed only by the water that cascades down the rocky face of the falls. As I approach, the mist catches the light and creates an ethereal veil between forest and falls.

I walk to the water's edge and let my bare toes caress the smooth pebbles.

It all looks exactly the same. But so much is different.

I am so different.

Chapter Three

KAYAN

 NE HUNDRED YEARS AGO

I WILL NEVER STOP BEING TRANSFIXED BY THE WAY HER freckles look in the moonlight. Not that she isn't beautiful in daylight, too. But like this . . . under the shadow of the trees that line the pool, she is incredible. Perhaps because this is one of her favourite places; one of the few places she can be still and quiet without the clamour of other peoples' feelings pressing down upon her.

"You know what amazes me about you?" I speak before I can stop myself, aware I sound like a soppy, lovesick young fae but unable to make myself care because tonight I *have* to tell her how I feel or I fear I might never be able to speak to her ever again. Even though I'm sure she knows – she's an empath, how could she *not* know? – I have to say it. I have to speak the words out loud, so I am not in any doubt about whether she reciprocates or not.

Alana stops, wriggling her toes into the gaps between the smooth pebbles on the shore. "My talent for skimming rocks?" She picks one up and throws it with perfect aim and skill so it skips and hops across the surface before disappearing a few feet in front of the falls.

I tilt my head and try to stifle a smile. So many in our village see her as weak, but I know the truth. She is strong – physically and mentally – and she has so much more power than she realises. "Well, there is that." I try to skim a stone and fail miserably. As it falters partway across the pond, I feel my wings flicker and the familiar swell of cool, tingling energy swirling in my veins – water *inside* my blood. Stepping stones of water bubble up to help my pebble all the way to the other side of the water.

"That's cheating." Alana frowns at me and folds her arms in front of her stomach.

"What amazes me," I say, scuffing my foot on the ground as I tuck my hands into my pockets, "is that I still feel like I'm finding out new things about you even after all this time." I look up, meeting her eyes. "We've known each other our entire lives. But you still surprise me, Alana."

For a moment, she holds my gaze, but then she tucks a strand of auburn hair behind her ear and turns away. Focusing her attention on the lake, she says, "I wish I could surprise everyone else."

A sigh makes her shoulders ripple. I want to reach out, put my arm around her, and pull her into a tight embrace. But I can't. That's not what we do.

Brushing the skirt of her dress, she sits down on the over-turned tree stump near the water's edge and braces her hands on her knees. "I've been trying to learn to control my magic," she says. "So I can choose when to read people and when not to."

I quirk an eyebrow at her. She has never spoken of her empathy as *magic* before. In fact, she has rarely spoken of it at all.

"The elders don't trust me," she says, a sigh making her shoulders droop. "Maura, especially, thinks empaths are bad news. I heard her saying as much to my father."

My jaw twitches. It's true, the elders are suspicious of Alana. They feel uncomfortable around her. As do many others.

"But if I can learn to control it – shut it off properly – then perhaps they'll feel more able to be around me."

There is a note of childlike desperation in Alana's voice that makes my gut twist with sadness. "Have you had any luck?"

She shakes her head. "I tried searching the books in my mother's library, but there isn't a single one that talks about how an empath can learn to channel their power or harness it. In fact, we're not really mentioned at all."

I tilt my head from side to side. "That kind of makes sense. You're the first empath in three hundred years to be born in the Leafborne community."

At this, Alana sighs and snaps, "I know. But surely, someone must know something that can help me?"

I sit down next to her and stretch out my feet, allowing the water to lap my toes. She's right, someone *should* help her. "Okay, look, I don't know anything about empaths. But I attended the academy for four years. I did my training. Maybe I can help."

Alana frowns at me for a moment, and then her frown turns into a smile. "You'd do that?"

I want to whisper, *I'd do anything for you.* But I don't. "Of course."

She pinches the bridge of her nose and closes her eyes. Sometimes, her freckles are so vibrant I'm convinced they'll smudge, like makeup, if she rubs them too hard.

"Maybe we just start with what they told us on our first day?" I think back to my first day at the academy. I remember missing Alana so deeply I thought I might quit, and run home, and be satisfied with never getting acquainted with my water affinity.

But I didn't.

"All right," she says, smiling and turning towards me as if I'm about to teach her the greatest lesson of all time.

"They told us magic comes from within. It's a part of who we are, intertwined with our very essence. It's powered by our emotions. So, we take the emotion we're feeling, latch onto it, and channel it —"

"I'm aware," she says. "You don't need to fae-splain it to me, Kayan."

I offer her an apologetic smile and swipe my fingers through my hair. "Sorry."

Alana shakes her head, laughing a little, although it's not a happy laugh. Even I know that, and I have no empathic abilities whatsoever.

She bites her lower lip and looks down at her fingers, which are fiddling with the fabric of her deep-burgundy-coloured skirt.

"What if it's different for me? What if my magic comes from everyone else's essence? Because honestly, Kayan, I don't feel it. When you all talk about your magic, you talk about the way it feels deep inside. As if it's a tangible, physical sensation. For me . . . it's just always there. Washing over me like waves. Sometimes calm and tranquil, sometimes tsunamis. But always there."

A little speechless, I stare out at the water and think about whether I can relate to what Alana's saying. As much as I try, I can't. My magic is part of me but separate from me. It's as if I'm a conduit for it. I feel it surging up inside me when I call to it, and at other times it lies dormant. Waiting to be used.

"Show me how you do it." Alana stands and moves towards the water.

"You've seen me do my party tricks a hundred times before," I tell her, even though part of me is dying to show off a little.

"Yes, but I'm not usually studying you," she says playfully. "This time, I'll watch carefully."

The twinkle in her eyes when she speaks makes my throat constrict, and knowing that she probably feels exactly how much I want her right now makes the sensation even harder to control. "Well," I shrug, "I do have *one* trick I haven't shown you. It took a long time to master. I haven't even shown the elders yet."

Alana's smile brightens. "I love a secret," she says.

Without speaking, I flex my wings and bend down to hitch up my pants so they're folded just below my knees. I stride into the water, allowing it to lap at my skin, welcoming me into its depths.

Alana remains in the shallows, the bottom of her dress damp from caressing the tops of the pebbles and the water that nestles between them.

I keep going until the water reaches the folded-up part of my pants, then stop and turn to face Alana. I tilt my head from side to side and stare at her.

What she doesn't know is that thinking of *her* is how I finally learned to master the most difficult aspect of my water magic; changing its form. Manipulating it into something else instead of simply moving it.

She meets my eyes, and the sensation that skids down my spine brings with it a surge of power. It settles in my legs, then spreads all the way back up to my fingertips. My wings flutter, and their powerful blue glow paints the surface of the water in glimmering shadows that stretch out like tendrils of light.

Tilting her head, Alana calls, "Tell me what you're doing. Talk me through it."

I inhale slowly, and try to vocalise what I'm feeling. "I'm focusing on happy thoughts," I tell her. "Happy feelings."

She nods in response.

"Latching on to the spark that lights in my belly, and willing it to intensify." I inhale sharply as my fingers twitch with the need to cast.

Alana looks down at her own fingers. Did she feel the same thing? If she is searching my emotions, then maybe . . .

"And now, I use it." I hold out my palm. A small, swirling bundle of blue light appears. I cast it into the air in front of me, then blow. Immediately, it turns from light to dust. A sparkling, brilliant blue dust that settles on the surface of the water.

As it meets the surface, there is a crackling sound. And another. And another.

I search deep down into the water below my feet, and use a cushion of it to bring me to the surface. As the rest of the lake turns to ice around me, I fly up into the air, hover, then land gently on the ice.

It meets the soles of my feet with a fierceness that takes my breath away.

I reach out to Alana and gesture for her to come to me.

The ice stops just in front of her feet. She hesitates, but then steps forward. When it holds her, and does not crack, she grins. Then she runs towards me, grabs my arms, and twirls around – the way we used to when we were kids and ice skating here in winter.

"Kayan, that's incredible." She is holding on to my elbows. "Incredible," she breathes, looking up at me.

I smile softly, and brush her cheek with my thumb. I am staring into her eyes, and she looks as though she's about to pull away. This is the moment. It has to be. "Alana . . . there's something I need to tell you. I think you know already, but I have to –"

She closes her eyes, and laces her fingers with mine. I have no idea if she's about to tell me she feels the same or that she's repulsed by the idea.

"I know," she whispers. "Of course, I know. I just always thought . . ." She trails off.

"Thought?"

Alana shakes her head and sighs. "I didn't want to ruin our friendship."

This time, I slip my arm around her waist and, with a graceful wave of my hand, snatch a piece of ice from the surface, return it to liquid in front of us, then catch the swirling droplets in mid-air and craft them into a delicate ice rose.

Alana looks at me and I nod for her to take it.

"It's yours."

Gently, with her thumb and forefinger, she takes hold of the stem and plucks the rose from the air. Studying it, she grins, and laughs joyfully. "Kayan . . ."

I step forward, trying to stride confidently, but skid on the ice and end up grabbing hold of her to steady myself.

Still holding her rose, she does not let go even when I have found my feet again.

I look into her eyes, and hers widen as if they are absorbing the rush of emotion that is surging through my body. "I love you, Alana. Always have. Always will."

Alana sighs a little. A content sigh, I think. Then brushes her thumb over the icy rose petals. She smiles up at me, then touches her thumb to my lips. It is cold, but that's not why my entire body is shivering. "Then kiss me," she breathes.

Chapter Four

ALANA

"*A*re you lost?" The stranger's voice drips through me like liquid silver.

I do not turn to face him. Instead, I keep watching the water and allowing the fury of the falls to fill my ears.

"Not lost. Alone." I steeple my fingers, close my eyes, and turn my face up to the sky – where a slowly rising moon smiles down on me.

"Very well." The stranger moves back through the undergrowth.

But I catch myself spinning around and saying, "Wait . . ."

I turn to look at him. He is still wearing his mask but my wings flutter as I take in his appearance. His gaze locks onto mine with a power that leaves me unable to move. His athletic frame is illuminated by the soft glow of the moonlight filtering through the trees. Around the mask, his hair is hidden by a hooded dark grey cloak that drifts down over his shoulders.

He takes a step closer, and I can't help but admire the way his loose silver pants hug his lean hips and the way his thick leather belt accentuates his toned abdomen.

Inside my gloves, my hands feel hot and my fingers twitch with the sudden, overwhelming need to touch him.

Is that my need? Or his?

I am so intoxicated by his gaze, I can barely tell which emotions are his and which are mine. Especially when I take in his bare, sculpted chest. Moving closer still, he smirks at me. I know he is smirking because I *feel* it – the arrogance in his swagger. The glint in his onyx eyes that tells me he is completely aware of the effect he is having on me.

A flush of warmth spreads through my body as I drink in the sight of him.

It has been so long since I allowed myself to feel this way about anyone – so long since I felt seen or wanted or desired – but somehow this man, this stranger, exudes a primal energy that turns my entire body to liquid.

I move closer, allowing myself to revel in the way it feels to be near him. Allowing the sensations to drown out the ache in my heart that settled there when I realised the man I once loved and my best friend are in love with each other.

Closing the distance between us, I keep my eyes fixed on his.

The air seems to crackle with anticipation. I search for his wings, trying to discover which element he is aligned to. But he has retracted them, and shows no signs of setting them free.

"Are you an empath?" I ask, the words slipping out before I have a chance to stop them.

He pauses. His fingers twitch at his sides as if he is resisting the urge to reach out and touch me. "No," he says. "But you are, *si'thari*. Aren't you?"

"*Si'thari?* You speak the old tongue?" I frown but he laughs.

"*Si'thari* – beautiful bird – is all I know. My older brother taught it to me to impress girls."

I laugh in return and shake my head. "It's working."

He tilts his head. "You didn't answer my question." His tone darkens.

Breathlessly, I nod. "Yes, I am an empath. Does that scare you?"

I worry the hem of my gloves. I yearn to have the warmth of his skin beneath my fingertips, to lose myself in the depths of those mesmerising eyes. But I can't.

I can fuck him, but I can't touch him.

"You do not scare me," he breathes. "You disarm me." His hand lands on my hip and squeezes tightly, jerking a surprised sigh from my chest.

"Do you know who I am?" I stare into his eyes, searching for the murky grey mist that will tell me he's lying.

"Varia," he says. And he means it.

I begin to smile. His fingers move from my hip to my face, and he traces the edge of my mask as I lean into his hand.

Intoxicating anticipation turns to fiery passion in my core. My heart races, my breath quickening as I wait for him to speak, to reveal more of himself to me. To tell me his name.

But he does not. Instead, he takes my hand, turns, and leads me towards the waterfall. We cross the rocks with ease. While I use my wings to keep myself steady, he uses just his balance and his quick-moving feet.

He tugs me behind it and pushes me up against the cold, slick rocks.

For a moment, I worry about the dress. But as soon as he touches me, the worry fades.

"I can't take off my mask," I tell him.

He brushes a firm thumb across my lower lip, then pauses while my tongue circles it. "Neither can I," he replies, watching me with a feral look in his eyes that makes my belly tingle.

I do not question him. I don't need to. All I need is whatever is about to happen next.

Dragging his thumb from my lips, down my neck, and between my breasts, he slips his other hand around my body to feel for the laces at the back of my dress.

"Leave it on," I tell him, meeting his eyes.

He blinks questioningly, but then nods. "As you say, *si'thari*. But your panties, at least, must come off or I won't be able to make you come."

The stranger's brazenness lights me on fire. I do not want this to be slow or sensual or romantic. I want it to be all the things I have not had for so many years. I want it to be heat, and desire, and sweat, and bodies, and pleasure. Pure, all-consuming pleasure.

Because even though I cannot touch him without a layer of fabric between us, he can touch me.

And *by the stars* does he touch me.

Tugging my underwear roughly down to my ankles, he makes me step out of them and tosses them aside. Then he slides his hands up the backs of my legs, caressing my calves and the backs of my knees with a feather-light touch that makes me sigh and tilt my hips towards him.

"You're so soft," he murmurs, lifting my dress and inching his fingers higher.

Reaching down, I scrape my fingers through his hair and bring his face closer to the apex of my thighs. I want to feel his tongue, and knowing I can't because of his mask makes me want it even more.

His fingers pause just short of my core, hovering, waiting to unleash their power. I can feel the heat emanating from his skin, the sweat that clings to his body, the strength it is taking for him not to speed up and devour me.

The smell of the forest, of dirt and damp leaves and earthy moss, mingles with the scent of his skin. The waterfall is loud, so loud it drowns out my thoughts until all I can think about is the way he is *not* touching me.

Gently, he strokes one finger through my wetness, starting at my clit and ending at my opening. He stops, makes a slow circle and then slides the tip of his finger inside me. As he does, my legs dip and a low moan escapes my lips.

He holds his finger there for torturous seconds, not moving, completely still.

When I brace a hand on his shoulder and ever-so-slightly tilt my pelvis, he tuts and roughly holds me still with his free hand.

I whimper and reach up to scrape my fingers through my hair.

Suddenly, I am desperate to free myself of my clothes. I want to feel the spray of the falls on my naked body. I want him to look up and worship me.

But then a second finger joins the first. After making a small torturous circle just inside my entrance, he growls and plunges them deep inside.

I cry out in a mixture of pain and pleasure as he curls his fingers forward while thrusting with a strength that makes the veins on his arms bulge and his breath hitch in his chest.

While he fucks me with his fingers, his other hand grips my thigh, holding me open for his exploration. A part of me is desperate to pull away, to escape from the intensity of it all, but it's too late – he is inside me, his fingers splayed wide as he thrusts them in and out in a frenzied rhythm that matches the pounding of my heart.

"Touch your clit while I fuck you," he commands, looking up at me.

"I don't just want your fingers," I murmur, grinding down onto his hand.

There's that smirk again – audible in his voice and tangible in the air. "Soon," he says. "But I want you to come for me first."

"Oh, fuck," I murmur, slipping my hand down to do as he says.

"Good girl," he whispers. "Show me how you like to be touched." He hesitates, then adds, "You want to keep those gloves on? Does the fabric feel good against your pussy?"

I whimper in response, unable to lie when I'm so completely trapped in the web of my own desire. But unable to tell him the truth either – that if I touch him when I'm losing control like this, I might break him.

I start to make frantic circles with three of my fingers, coaxing throbbing, trembling pleasure from my pussy.

As the stranger sits back a bit on his knees so he can watch me, still fucking me with his fingers, he studies my hand like he's trying to learn the exact pattern and rhythm that will take me over the edge.

My orgasm approaches, the pressure building deep inside my body. I lean forward and brace my weight on his shoulder, my knees becoming weak. "It's okay," he mutters, "I can take it. Use me."

My nails dig into his naked back, but he hardly seems to notice. His eyes are black with desire, and I can feel the sheer force of his arousal coursing through every movement.

"Keep going, please."

"You're in control," he says. "I won't stop unless you tell me to stop."

He continues his relentless thrusting, each movement driving me further into a swirling inferno of desire. My heart beats so wildly I feel like it's about to crack my ribs.

I cry out again, desperate for more.

Without missing a beat, he keeps fucking me while I rub my clit. I release a loud, unrestrained cry of pleasure. It mixes with the torrents of water running down the rock face beside us and echoes off the damp walls of the cave. As I uncoil for him, the way he wants me, he wraps around my limbs and squeezes me tight, putting me back together even as I fall apart.

Shaking, I collapse forward, body trembling uncontrollably with the force of my climax. My skin feels electrified, every nerve lighting up with pleasure. But he catches me. He holds me steady, then pulls me down into his arms and keeps me close while I return to my body.

"*Si'thari*, you are incredible," he whispers against my ear, his voice muffled from inside his mask.

"So are you." I run my fingers through his hair, desperate to take off his mask. Smiling, I stroke his earlobe and he leans into my touch. "If I can't see you, I should at least know your name."

He looks up at me and something flickers around him. Sadness. Frustration.

I feel as if he is about to speak when something shatters the moment.

It is a scream. Distant. Somewhere beyond the falls. But it is not a scream of pleasure.

I stand quickly and run to the entrance of the cave. More screams. And then . . . a wave of pure, unadulterated fear hits me smack in the chest. It is so forceful I almost collapse back to the floor. There is another, then another. A tsunami of terror pummelling through me so hard I can barely breathe.

"Something bad is happening," I whisper. "We have to go."

But when I turn around, the stranger has already gone.

Chapter Five

ALANA

I run, my heart pounding in my chest, my breath coming in short, sharp gasps. The screams grow louder as I approach the bonfire, fear congealing in my chest and my temples.

Not just mine . . . everyone's.

My dress tangles around my legs, but I push forward, driven by a sickening sense of dread, trying to slam the gates of my empathy back down so I can at least see through the blinding fog of chaos and figure out what is happening.

As I break through the tree line, I rip the mask from my face and throw it to the ground. The scene in front of me steals all the air from my lungs. Dark, bulky figures move through the crowd, their faces obscured by grotesque masks, their hands wielding chains and weapons.

I know these figures, but only from the twisted tales we were told as children.

Fae traders. Gloomweavers.

My wings shudder, and dread drips down my spine. I rise into the air. I have barely reached the lower branches of the nearest tree when something whizzes past me, pain strikes my leg, and I drop to the ground.

Stunned, I stare up at the dark canopy. My legs are hot. I smell smoke. It swirls around me, but I can't figure out where it is coming from until someone shouts, "She's on fire!"

I look down, and realise they're right. My dress has caught light.

As fiery arrows fly through the air all around me, I roll over and over, wrapping my wings around myself and crying out as they absorb the heat that burns me. Finally, the fire is extinguished. I rise unsteadily to my feet. My ears are ringing, and my leg feels tingly and numb. I pull up my dress and see a large, red wound on my thigh. Not from fire, from something else.

I stumble forward, then someone catches my elbow. "Alana . . ." Kayan appears at my side. His eyes widen as he takes me in. He sees me. My heart flutters but then another scream breaks through the undergrowth. Blood curdling. Death.

"Alana!" Another voice. Rosalie. She runs towards me full pelt.

There was a time when the three of us were friends. There was a time when I thought she would be at my side when Kayan and I pledged our lives to one another. Now it is she who he clings to, letting me go and turning to pull her into his arms.

My dress is singed. The enchantments have been broken by the fire, but none of that matters now. What matters is . . . "We have to get out of here."

"What's happening?" Rosalie looks from me to Kayan.

"They've come for us. Gloomweaver. Fae traders." I meet her eyes, willing her not to argue with me for perhaps the first time in her life. Feeling as though not a moment has passed since the three of us used to mock, and cajole, and adore each other.

A confused laugh escapes Rosalie's perfectly pink lips. "But they're just stories," she whispers. "No one has ever seen them in real life."

Ignoring her, I scan the crowd desperately, searching for the elders. For Rawk. For anyone who could take charge and get us to safety. But faces blur together in a sea of panic and confusion.

Fae run and fly in every direction, their screams piercing the night air, their wings fluttering uselessly as nets sizzling with dark magic slam down on top of them.

Some try to fight.

But they fall like flies, dropping to the ground as they are hit by arrows that quite literally drain the colour from their wings and the life from their bodies.

I look down at my gloved hands. I have no powers that can help. I have no elemental abilities. I can cast spells and enchantments, and read people's emotions, but I can't *fight*. Even if I pulled off my gloves, I'd have no idea how to replicate what I did to Kayan when we were –

"Rosalie, can you create a wall of fire around us? Protect us?" Kayan grips Rosalie's forearms.

Her eyes dazzle and she nods quickly at him. But she has barely raised her hands when her eyes widen and her fingers fly to her throat. An iron collar snaps closed around her neck. Kayan lunges towards her, but he is caught, too.

And then it is my turn.

I feel the cold bite of iron around my neck. It constricts against my throat. I pull at it and try to break free but a rough voice says, "It's pointless to try and resist."

A face appears in front of me. Masked at first, but then he pulls his mask free, grabs hold of me, and leans in so close that I can smell his cabbagey breath and feel its heat on my cheek. He has scarred, pockmarked skin. Yellow teeth. Huge, bulky shoulders. No wings. Gloomweavers are not fae; they are something else entirely.

My captor licks his lips, spittle bubbling in the crevice at the corner of his mouth as he looks me up and down. "Well, well, well," he drools. "What a pretty one I have here."

Beside us, two more traders grab hold of Kayan and Rosalie and start to drag them away.

For a moment, I imagine the stranger from the waterfall might appear and slit the Gloomweaver's throat. Leap onto his back, slash at his neck, grab my hand and set me free.

I have barely finished imagining when everything goes dark. A rough sack is yanked over my head, pulled down, and fastened tight around my thrashing wings, bending them in ways they are not supposed to bend, bringing tears of pain to my eyes.

Darkness engulfs me. My wings strain against the confines of the sack. But it's useless. I'm lifted off the ground, my body thrown over a broad shoulder like a sack of grain. The scent of sweat and leather fills my nostrils, and I gag, my stomach churning.

I'm carried through the forest, the sounds of the raid fading behind me, replaced by the heavy thud of boots on damp earth. My captor moves swiftly but with the gait of a person who is not used to traversing the forests.

We should have outsmarted them. On any other night, we could have escaped them with ease. But our magic was focused on the ceremony. On our costumes and cele-brations.

We were naive, and distracted, and now the Leafborne are about to become no more.

For I am almost certain no one escaped.

AFTER WHAT FEELS LIKE AN ETERNITY, I'M TOSSED unceremoniously onto something hard and wooden. My body slams against the rough surface and I lie there, gasping for breath, my heart racing as I strain to hear the voices around me.

"Kayan? Is that you?" It's Rawk, his voice tight with fear.

"I'm here." Kayan's reply is strained. "But Rosalie . . ." He swallows hard, and I can picture his shoulders sagging with the weight of not being able to protect her. "I lost her. I kept calling for her, and for a while she answered but –"

"Who else?" Rawk barks, taking roll call of those who are here too. "Can anyone use their magic?"

A series of tiny fizzing noises fill the confines of our enclosure. "Something is stopping it," says one of the elders. "Dark magic. It is thick in this place. Can't you all feel it?"

"Yes," says Rawk. "I feel it."

"And all this time we thought traders were the stuff of story and legend," the elder replies. "We were blind. Arrogant. Stupid."

"Enough," Rawk mutters. "Lamenting our failings will not set us free." He might not be an elder yet but, in this brief moment, he almost sounds like one.

There is a long, heavy silence as the weight of our situation settles in the air. Then the wagon – for I assume it's a wagon we've been loaded into – jolts and begins to move.

"What about Alana? She was with us," Kayan says quietly.

"I'd have thought you'd relish in the idea of her meeting her end on a night like this," Rawk replies. I can hear the bloodlust in his voice. "A bittersweet irony, no?"

"No," Kayan bites back. "I would not *relish* in it, Rawk."

"Ohhh, Kayan. Always so righteous. Even though you are nothing but a shell. Lesser than even a Shadowkind fae, these days. Utterly, pathetically, useless."

"Please . . ." I speak without meaning to. "Stop."

There is a pregnant pause, and then Kayan says, "Alana?"

"Yes, it's me. I'm here."

"You left your cabin?" Rawk asks, as if only just realising that Kayan said he and Rosalie were with me.

I hesitate, fear burning hot on my cheeks. "Yes. I left."

Rawk lets out a loud laugh, like a clap of thunder. "Of course, you did. Probably led them to us." Even with my gates up, I can feel the vitriol in his seething muscles.

"I would never –"

"Quiet." Rawk's voice fills the entire wagon. "Shut your fucking mouth, and let me think of how to get us out of this."

I press my lips together. I am desperate to remove my mask, and my gloves, and to *see* what is happening. But I can't. I am bound, like the others, and the collar around my neck makes me feel like I can't breathe.

Tonight was supposed to bring me freedom. A few short hours ago, I was free. I was soaring above myself, feeling the most alive I have in years.

But now it is all over.

"Did anyone see a stranger tonight? He was wearing a blood-red mask." I raise my voice, ignoring Rawk's instruction because here – now – he is not my superior. None of them are.

No one replies.

"Someone must have seen him. He wasn't from our village. At least, I didn't recognise him." Still, no one replies. It is as if I haven't spoken. As if, even now when we face the same horrible fate, I am still a pariah.

"I didn't see him," Kayan whispers. "Do you think he had something to do with the raid?"

I shake my head, even though no one can see me doing so. "No, I just . . ." I screw my eyes shut in the darkness and try to bite back the tears that are rising in my throat. "He disappeared in the chaos and I'm worried, that's all."

"We're all worried about someone," snaps one of the older women.

"Does she still have her gloves on?" mutters someone else. Then to me, "Do you still have your gloves on?"

I shift uncomfortably. My wings throb and my shoulder aches from being pinned at a strange angle. Even now, when we are in the grip of a hoard of fae traders, they are afraid of me.

"Are you all right?" Kayan asks quietly.

An ironic smile curves the corners of my mouth. "I have been thinking about tonight for so long," I sigh. "I thought I finally had a chance to escape from myself." I shake my head, my neck aching, and stare at the pitch-dark insides of my prison. "Seems I've managed to do the opposite – I'm trapped here with the very worst version of myself. The version they all see."

"Not all," Kayan says gently. "Alana . . ."

"Quiet!" the voice of the Gloomweaver who carried me through the forest booms into the darkness. "The next faerie who speaks will find themselves missing a tongue in the morning."

My body aches. My wings are cramped and sore from being bound for what feels like an eternity. Two days have passed since the raid, two days of rattling along rough roads, being denied food and given only a few sips of water.

A while ago, just after midday, we entered the city. The air changed. It grew thick with smoke, and sweat, and bodies, and dust. Already, I crave air. Real air that is thick with dew, and moss, and life.

The air here is thick with nothing but death.

Finally, the wagon jolts to a stop.

As the Gloomweavers bark orders and the wagons are unloaded, I strain to hear the sounds around me. The clatter of hooves on cobblestones, the distant shouts of merchants hawking their wares, the pungent smell of sewage and unwashed bodies. There is only one place we can be; Luminael the capital city of Veridia. A place that was once bright, and ethereal, and full of magic which, under the rule of Lord Eldrion – the oldest fae in the kingdom – has fallen to ruin.

Amid the cacophony, a sickening realisation dawns on me. "They're going to sell us," I whisper, my voice hoarse and ragged. "Eldrion's slaving district . . . that's where they're taking us. We've all heard the stories about how he wants to rid the outer regions of elemental fae."

"Quiet," Rawk hisses, but I can hear the fear in his voice. For years, we've heard tales of Eldrion's family. The fae who have become ever more cruel with each generation, turning Luminael into a place where Sunborne fae like him rule supreme.

To the others, a little softer, he says, "I won't let that happen. We'll find a way out."

A jolt of laughter parts my lips. "How? We're bound, powerless. Fighting will only make it worse."

Rawk doesn't reply.

Silence descends, broken only by the thud of footsteps and the clank of chains as we're dragged from the wagon. I stumble, my legs weak and unsteady, but rough hands grip my arms, hauling me forward.

We're thrown into cells, the iron bars slamming shut with a deafening clang. I hear Kayan inhale sharply as his sack is ripped away; I'd know his breath anywhere.

"What are those?" he asks, panic lacing his tone.

"Magic binders," a gruff voice replies. "Don't want any faerie tricks ruining our plans."

Kayan falls quiet. There is a clicking sound as, I assume, his collar is removed and replaced by the cuffs. The same voice says, "Strip," and there follows a hiss of water and Kayan's grunt of pain.

Barely a moment later, my own sack is yanked off, and I blink in the dim light, my eyes struggling to adjust. I catch a glimpse of Kayan, naked and shivering, before a pair of pale brown pants are tossed at his feet and he's chained to the wall.

The others huddle near the doors. Perhaps twenty of us, which means the rest of the village is . . . where?

I am trying to count, trying to see if I recognise anyone's feet or lower limbs when the slaver who kidnapped me steps out of the shadows. His lips stretch into a wide, spittle-laced grin. Dangling a key in front of me, he unfastens my collar and lets it drop to the ground. I rub my neck, my skin sighing with relief.

The Gloomweaver leers, his eyes roaming my body with undisguised hunger even though I'm still fully clothed. "Those gloves," he says, reaching for my hands. "Take them off."

Panic surges through me, even though it wouldn't be a bad thing if I took this slaver's mind and broke it.

From the huddle of bodies, I hear Rawk's bitter tone. "Trust me," he mutters, "you don't want her to do that."

"And why's that?" The Gloomweaver stalks over to Rawk, tugging on the hood that still covers his face and torso.

"Because she's a freak," Rawk spits. "She'll sap the energy from you if she touches you." He jerks his head in Kayan's direction. "She did it to him. Sucked out his magic. Took him twenty years to find his mind again. And now, he can't even fly."

"Rawk, what are you doing?" someone hisses. "Stop telling them things."

"Listen," Rawk says, pushing back his shoulders even though they're bound. "I can handle her. You treat me with a little more respect and I'll help you make sure she's an asset, not a deadly waste of space."

Bile swills in my stomach.

There's a long pause, then the Gloomweaver hawks saliva into his mouth, spits on the floor, and says, "Fine, but one wrong move and you're faerie dust."

Roughly, he tugs the sack over Rawk's head.

"I said . . . respect." Rawk meets his eyes.

The Gloomweaver tuts, then offers a sarcastic smile before gently fastening magic binders onto Rawk's wrists. "Now," he says, jerking his head at me. "Get those gloves off her and put these on instead." He dangles an identical pair of magic binders in front of Rawk's face.

Rawk narrows his eyes but smiles, then turns to me.

He approaches me slowly.

Standing in front of me, he moistens his lower lip in a way that makes me want to rip his skin from his scalp and burn it in the fire.

"Try anything, and you're dead," he whispers.

"Why are you doing this?" I hiss. "Are you really going to work with them? Do you think they'll extend you any grace? Do you think –"

An unexpected slap across the face makes me cry out. Rawk stares at me, hand still raised as if he's preparing to strike me again, his eyes blazing.

The Gloomweaver chuckles darkly.

No one else speaks.

"Keep still." Eyeing the flush of pink that blooms across my cheek, Rawk slides the gloves from my hands and drops them to the floor. Instantly, the Gloomweaver notices the cuffs that are already on my wrists and strides forward. "What are those?"

"They were to prevent her from changing at the Forest Moon." Rawk shrugs. "Sadly, they don't stop all magic."

"Get them off her," the Gloomweaver spits.

Rawk nods, then mutters an incantation over the cuffs. When they do not fall away, he turns to the Gloomweaver and says, "I need my magic to take them off. I was the one who gave them to her. Only my enchantment can unfasten them."

The Gloomweaver sighs loudly, rolls his eyes, then unfastens the magic binders on Rawk's wrists. "Be quick," he spits.

Rawk turns back to me. He meets my eyes. And in that second, suddenly, I know what he's planning to do. I give a quick shake of my head, but as my cuffs fall away, Rawk spins around. Bright white light blooms in his hands. He roars and throws it at the Gloomweaver, his wings expanding and filling the space between them as he rises up into the air.

Like this, I see why he was on the path to becoming an elder. He is powerful, and magnificent.

The Gloomweaver has landed on his back, but springs to his feet and draws a dagger from his waist.

"You think a dagger can protect you?" Rawk laughs. "We were caught off guard but our magic —" his eyes widen. He looks down at his chest.

An arrow has pierced his skin. His wings falter. He dips in the air, tries to stay alight, then dips again and crumples on the floor. He blinks, coughing as blood pools at the corner of his mouth.

A second Gloomweaver steps out of the shadows, shaking her head and tutting, holding a bow and a clutch of arrows. "I knew one of them would try something," she says, helping up the one Rawk knocked to the floor.

"Rawk . . ." I breathe.

Some of the others, still tied up and blinded by the cloth sacks they wear, begin to cry.

Rawk coughs again as the Gloomweaver stands over him. He reaches down, takes hold of the arrow, then leans on it. Rawk releases a gut-wrenching moan, and writhes beneath the Gloomweaver's weight as the arrow burrows deeper into his chest. "You forest folk really are as stupid as you look," he spits.

Then he pulls the arrow free, kicks Rawk onto his stomach, and steps over him to get to me. "You were smart not to fight," he says, motioning for me to extend my arms.

I cannot speak.

Nodding, the Gloomweaver fixes the magic binders onto me, then picks my gloves back up and pulls them down over my hands. "Now take the rest off," he says, raising an eyebrow.

I can't breathe. Can't move.

"Or I'll do it for you." He reaches for me and I flinch, backing away and reaching around to unlace my dress. It falls into a pool around my ankles, and he quickly picks up a hose and sprays me down. Ice-cold water stings my skin, freezes my thoughts, leaves me shivering and unable to speak.

When he shoves a pale brown dress into my hands, he stands back to watch me put it on. It has barely dropped past my hips when he grabs my arm, tugs me to the wall, and chains me beside Kayan.

I stumble to step over Rawk's legs as he moves me.

"Alana . . ." Kayan tries to meet my gaze but I can't look at him.

"I'm all right," I whisper. But I'm not all right. None of us are.

One by one, the others are processed, stripped of their dignity and their freedom. When it's done, the slavers leave, their laughter echoes through the halls, and the cell falls quiet.

"What do you think happened to Rosalie?" Kayan whispers.

I swallow hard. "Perhaps she escaped."

There is a long pause, then Kayan whispers, "You don't believe that, do you?"

I do not answer him; the truth will do us no favours tonight.

Chapter Six

ELDRION

*B*elow, Luminael descends into the gloom of yet another twilight. I have seen too many nights in this city, yet it is mine to command. So, I cannot leave it.

Once a shining beacon of all that was good in the kingdom, the city now lies in a state of decay and despair. Even from this height, I can smell the stench of poverty and hopelessness wafting up from the slums.

It was not always this way. There was a time when Luminael was a place of beauty and enchantment, when fae of all kinds flocked to its gleaming spires and lush gardens. But that was long ago, before the world turned cold and cruel, before the darkness began to creep in.

A knock on the door interrupts my brooding thoughts. "Enter," I call out, not bothering to turn around.

The door creaks open and I tighten my grip on my whisky glass.

"My lord . . ."

I sigh and pinch the bridge of my nose. "What is it, Finn?"

The jester has a habit of interrupting me when I most want to be alone. When he doesn't answer, I turn around, allowing my large black wings to unfurl, understanding exactly how intimidating they are for a Shadowkind who has no magic and stunted wings.

Dipping his head low and bending his body into a bow, Finn mutters, "I bring news from the outskirts."

I pace towards him. "News?"

Finn swallows hard, and looks up at me from beneath his mask. "There has been an incident, my lord. One of the forest villages was raided by the Gloomweavers. They . . . they took all of the fae."

I frown. "An entire village?" Then I chuckle. "The Gloomweavers are getting brave."

"My lord —"

I wave a dismissive hand. "The forest folk are nothing to me, and we need the Gloomweavers to keep trade moving in the city. The trade in lower born fae is something that has sustained us for generations." I narrow my eyes, taking in the piercings on Finn's wings that tell the story of his centuries-long servitude to my family.

"Yes, Lord Eldrion but —" he swallows forcefully and draws himself up. From beneath his dark mask, his eyes snag on mine and cause me to allow him to speak.

"My lord, it was Alana's village. She was one of them."

Her name hits me like a physical blow. Alana. I turn slowly to face Finn, my eyes blazing with a fury that makes him cower. "What did you say?"

"Alana, my lord," he repeats, his voice barely above a whisper. "She was among those taken."

"Alana is with the Gloomweavers?"

Finn nods, steepling his fingers together and worrying his lower lip with his teeth. "I believe she will be traded at tomorrow's market."

Fury erupts like a volcano deep inside me. I fly at him, throw my hand around his throat and squeeze until he chokes out a stifled, "Lord Eldrion, please. I thought you'd want to know."

Dropping him so hard he falls to the floor, I turn around and stride back to the window. "Get out," I growl, my hands clenching into fists at my sides. "Get out, now."

Finn scurries from the room but I barely hear him go.

I pace the length of the throne room, my wings twitching. With a roar of frustration, I slam my fist against the window pane, sending cracks splintering across the glass.

The Gloomweavers can do what they will with the rest of the elementals. They can strip the forests bare, and the valleys, and the beaches. But Alana is mine.

She is mine, and I will do what I must to claim her.

Chapter Seven

ALANA

I wake with a start, my neck screaming in protest as I lift my head from where it lolled against my chest during the night. The chains around my wrists dig into my skin. I can't believe I fell asleep. It must have been sometime in the early hours, when the sound of the others crying became too much to bear. Even with my gates up.

My mouth is dry, and my tongue sticks to the roof of my mouth.

As my eyes adjust to the dim light, I see Rawk's lifeless body still sprawled on the floor and wish I was still sleeping.

"Would have been easier if he'd stayed an asshole right up to the end, huh?" Kayan says, his chains clinking as he shifts to look at me.

I offer him a wry smile. My hair has fallen across my face, but moving it is awkward because of the chains. "Don't worry about Rosalie," I offer him. "She'll be fine. She's feisty."

He smiles, and his cheek dimples. "She certainly is." He inhales sharply, looking at me as though he's about to say something important. But then the cell door clangs open, and the bulky silhouettes of the Gloomweavers appear on the other side of the bars.

Rough hands grab at us, dragging us to our feet. I don't recognise these ones, but it doesn't matter. They are all as cruel as each other.

They herd us out of the cell, prodding us with the butts of their weapons, their laughter echoing off the stone walls as we pass through dark, dank tunnels.

We emerge into a vast, circular space, a colosseum-like structure with tiered seats rising up on all sides. The light stings my eyes, and I squint up at the stands as thick, humid air meets my skin.

The stands are filled with a raucous crowd, drinking and hollering despite the fact the sun is only just creeping up over the horizon.

"Eldrion lets this happen?" Kayan hisses at me. "I mean, he must know about it, and he lets it happen?"

I shake my head and sigh. Over the years, I've become good at listening. When no one speaks to you, it is about the only thing you can do. And I've heard the rumours. I've heard what they say about the lord who rules Luminael. About his cruelty, the way he treats women, the backhanders he gives to criminals and thugs in order to keep the streets under control.

The elders keep it from the rest of the villagers. But they know what happens in the cities and, because of them, I know too.

"Why would he care what happens here?" I ask with a sigh. "Sunborne care for no one but themselves, and he is the oldest of them all. To him, elementals are bugs to be squashed. Not because we are inferior like the Shadowkind, but because he is afraid of us."

Kayan hisses through his front teeth. Before he can answer me, we are thrust into a pen at one side of the arena, our chains rattling as we collide with each other in the tight space.

Across from us, a stage rises from the dirt floor, and upon it stands the female Gloomweaver who ended Rawk's life. She raises her hands, and the crowd falls silent.

"Welcome," she calls out, her voice ringing through the arena. "Today, we have a special treat for you. A fresh batch of forest fae, ripe for the picking."

My stomach churns at her words, bile rising in my throat. Beside me, Kayan tenses, his jaw clenched tight.

The Gloomweaver gestures to the side of the stage. The crowd falls silent, and then my heart leaps into my throat as Rosalie is dragged forward, her hair tangled and matted, her face streaked with tears. Kayan's entire body uncoils and he lurches forward. A guard nearby slashes at his shins with a large metal prod, then smashes it across his back, striking his wings and sending him to his knees.

Rosalie stands, trembling, in the same pale brown dress I was given to wear. She searches the crowd, then her eyes land on the pen. She cannot see Kayan because he is still on the floor, but she sees me. Her eyes catch mine.

I nod at her and try to smile. Try to tell her it will be all right if she stays strong.

Oh, how I wish I could take her pain away. Absorb it all, swallow it down, and leave her feeling brave and powerful instead of like she's about to crumble.

Something stirs in my stomach; the urge to let my gates down and search out Rosalie's feelings. But what good would that do? I wouldn't just let hers in, I'd let in the swirling, cacophonous emotions of every soul in the arena.

I am still trying to fight the urge to feel for her when the Gloomweaver launches into a rapid-fire sales pitch, extolling Rosalie's virtues as a breeder and her abilities as a fire faerie. The crowd grows restless, shouting out bids.

In the end, it is a rotund man with a leering grin and a pair of golden Sunborne wings who claims her, his bid outstripping all others. Rosalie sobs quietly as she is dragged away.

In front of me, Kayan's shoulders shake as he starts to sob too.

I drop to my knees beside him, my heart breaking for him. "Shh," I whisper, stroking his hair. "We'll find a way out of this. We'll find her."

But even as I say the words, I know they are hollow. How can we find her when we're about to be sent to our own version of the hell she is headed for?

As the auction continues, as more of our kin are torn away from us, sold to the highest bidder, a numbness settles over me. This cannot be happening, cannot be real.

Any minute now, I'll wake up in the cave behind the waterfall. The stranger in the blood-red mask will be there, cradling me in his arms. And everything will be right again.

I close my eyes, trying to block out the sights and sounds of the arena.

It works.

The noise dies down, and something in the air shifts. Quiet descends. For a moment, I feel like I can breathe again. But then I open my eyes to see every single fae in the arena staring in the same direction.

At the side of the stage, a huge, looming shadow has appeared. The Gloomweaver running the auction flexes her fingers on her wooden staff and takes a step back. She looks afraid. Everyone looks afraid.

And then I realise why.

"Lord Eldrion, what a pleasure." The Gloomweaver dips into a bow as the tallest fae I've ever seen steps out of the shadows.

My mouth becomes instantly dry, and my wings stiffen.

Eldrion's presence commands the entire arena. A simmering column of power, he strides towards the Gloomweaver. His wings, huge and black, iridescent onyx in the morning sun, unfurl at his sides, casting shadows over the stage.

As he moves, his long, silver hair catches the light, cascading down his back like a river of molten metal. His chiselled features are sharp and angular, with high cheek-bones and a strong jawline that could have been carved from marble.

He is beautiful. And he is deadly. A lord and a predator.

"I was not invited to this morning's auction," he says in a

timbre that is deep and rough. He raises an eyebrow and folds his arms in front of his expansive chest.

The Gloomweaver stutters nervously. "I wasn't aware . . ." She trails off, then corrects herself. "An unforgivable error on my part, Lord Eldrion. How may I make it up to you?"

Is she flirting with him? On stage? While we are sold like cattle?

Eldrion does not bite. Instead, he turns and fixes his gaze on the pen where we are being held. "This is all that is left?" he asks, waving a casual hand in our direction.

The Gloomweaver nods. "Yes, my lord."

He nods slowly and then, causing a ripple of shock to move through the crowd, flies over the heads of the audience and lands with a thud in front of us.

Dust flies up from the ground.

His wings beat hard against the sticky, congealed air of the arena, and his ice-like eyes scan our faces. When they graze across mine, something tugs at my belly. A quiver of treacherous intrigue that makes me want to lower my head in shame.

Except, I can't. Because he is staring at me and I cannot look away.

Although his head barely moves, I feel his eyes trace my features. He takes in my hair, my pale skin, the freckles on the bridge of my nose. He looks at my wings, my arms, and the gloves I wear.

Then he snaps his gaze away, flies back to the stage and says, "I'll take them all. Name your price."

The Gloomweaver's eyebrows jerk up towards her hairline. "All, my lord?" She laughs nervously. "It's just that I have customers expecting –"

"Are you refusing me, Gloomweaver?" Eldrion's voice booms like thunder, shaking the stone walls of the arena.

Every single person holds their breath.

The Gloomweaver shakes her head. "No, of course not, my lord. They are yours. You just pay me what you see fit. Take them . . ." She gestures in our direction. "Take them all."

"Very well." Eldrion reaches into his pocket, takes out a small velvet purse, and throws it to her feet. Then he snaps his fingers and, from the sides of the arena, a flurry of royal guards appear.

The pen is opened, and we are dragged out, hustled towards the door, through the dark underbelly of the arena, then out into the light again.

Eldrion does not appear again until, two hours later, after being marched through the streets of Luminael, we arrive at the citadel. On a small island, it is accessible only by foot at low tide because – legend says – Eldrion's guards will shoot down any fae who dares attempt to fly over its walls.

My pace slows as I look up at it. Home to the upper echelons of Sunborne society, it rises dramatically from the wet sand at its roots. According to books from my mother's library, within the thick stone walls, a maze of winding streets and tightly packed buildings climb up towards the central keep. And at the island's pinnacle sits the ancient castle itself. Eldrion's castle.

From here, we can just about see the spires that stretch up towards the clouds.

"Keep moving," a guard barks roughly.

We do as he says, our bare feet meeting the cool, wet sand and sighing with relief after so long without proper rest.

It is almost midday by the time we reach the castle. The climb through the narrow streets was arduous. Seeing us coming, Sunborne nobility slammed their doors and windows closed, leaving us to crawl our way towards the man who purchased us with tired legs and aching lungs.

No one speaks as we walk, and it is only when the castle comes into view that I hear Kayan say, "Holy stars, I didn't think I'd ever lay eyes on this place."

I catch him glancing at me, and exhale slowly. The castle looks nothing like the pictures I have seen. It sits high up, yes, but instead of glimmering resplendently as the sun catches its curves and lines, it looms like a sinister sentinel watching over the city. Its once bright walls are now scuffed and muted. Dark. Too dark.

A shudder racks my body.

Something feels different here.

Yes, the outer districts of Luminael felt dirty, and chaotic, and insidiously dark. But this is different. Even with the gates of my affinity locked down tightly, I cannot help but feel the desperation that hangs in the air here.

As my wings flutter violently, a guard tells me to keep still. "You fly, you die," he reminds me, jerking his eyes up towards the parapet of the castle where Eldrion's soldiers wait with glinting arrows.

Thinking of the arrows, my thigh burns. I was not hit with enough of the Gloomweaver's poison to be killed by it, but I am afraid it is spreading slowly through my body because the wound is starting to feel hot and painful beneath my dress.

As we approach the castle gates, I crane my neck to take in the full scope of the building. It is a testament to Eldrion's power, a physical manifestation of the iron grip his family have had on Luminael and the wider kingdom for thousands of years.

But, still, I cannot escape that feeling. The one that tells me there is something bigger and more sinister at play here.

We are on the bridge approaching the large wooden doors when something moves. A shadow. Above us.

I look up, and at first I think it is a gargoyle staring down at me.

Then I realise it is him. Eldrion. His ink-black wings tucked behind him, he stares down from the tallest spire, watching us.

Watching me.

Chapter Eight

ELDRION

She is here. This is not how it was supposed to happen. But she is here, and she cannot escape me. Not now. Not without magic.

I watch from the roof as she is herded through the gates. While the other Leafborne look terrified, she shines like a beacon of defiance.

She may not know it, may not *feel* it, but she is the personification of power. Her hair, her wings, the way she carries herself. As if she will not be beaten. It is both captivating and infuriating because it seems she has no idea who I am or what I am capable of. Which means I will be forced to show her.

Striding over to the fireplace, I mutter an incantation that will fan the flames. They surge, glow bright white, then soften back to orange and continue to flicker in the grate.

There is a knock on the door. I know it is Briony even before she says, "My lord? You called for me?"

"Enter."

Leaning against the mantle with my forearm, I purposefully do not look at the maid. I have known her too long, and she knows me too well. Her family were sold to mine six centuries ago. And while her father and brothers had to be extinguished, she has always been loyal to a fault.

I trust her.

And that is an unnerving sensation.

"We have guests arriving," I say darkly. "One of them – a female Leafborne – is to be given her own chambers. She is . . ." I hesitate, unsure how to phrase my intentions, "special to me, Briony."

Now, I do turn around.

Briony is standing by the door, small wings tightly folded against her back, dark eyes watching me.

"Do you understand?"

She nods, swallowing forcefully. "I believe so, my lord."

"I am entrusting her to you. You're to serve her. See she's fed and clothed. She can travel freely throughout the castle but she cannot leave." I walk slowly towards the petite Shadowkind. "You will ensure she understands that attempting to leave is futile?"

Briony casts her eyes down to her forearms. While hers are bare and untarnished, there are many here who bear the marks of escape attempts. I allow them one chance – one opportunity to explore just how hopeless their situation is – before I dish out a final, fatal punishment.

"I will make sure she understands, my lord." Briony hesitates. She worries her fingers together and glances towards the table where my whisky sits. "And you, my lord? Will you be eating this evening?"

I turn away from her, growling deep in the back of my throat. "I will not."

"May I speak freely, my lord?" Briony's voice trembles.

"You may not." I pick up a glass, pour some whisky, and gesture to the door. "What you may do is leave me. Henrik knows which rooms I have assigned my guest. Have him give you the key."

There is a pause, which always follows after I mention Henrik's name in Briony's presence. But I do not interrogate it. Although I forbid the Shadowkind from fornicating under my roof, it is the one area in which I tend to show leniency; they need *something* to keep their spirits from breaking.

"Very good, my lord." Briony exits quietly, and I wait until her footsteps have disappeared down the hall before sighing loudly.

Although my chambers are located in a secluded part of the castle, even they are beginning to feel too much. Dimly lit by flickering lanterns, there are rich tapestries on the walls – inherited from my parents – and a perpetual scent of old books in the air. They used to bring me comfort. I used to revel in my solitude, catching snatches of it between banquets and meetings with the Sunborne courtiers.

But ever since I found out about *her*, I have come to hate them more and more.

She infects my thoughts. Visions of her torment my mind day and night.

And there is no escape.

Except . . .

I stride over to the door and throw the bolts across it. Then I close my eyes and mutter the incantation that will bring the past into the present.

"*Mael'kor vistrae, ekan'thar nost'rae. Shar'il minae, thaes'kor nost'rae . . .*"

The air begins to shimmer, then it parts like a scissor cut in a piece of fabric, a large black hole forming in front of my eyes. Bracing myself, I step through it. Into the memory.

It is dark here too, but I wait, knowing there will soon be a flicker of heat in the corner of the room.

Sure enough, there it is. Fire blooms in the grate, and the rest of the room materialises slowly. A cabin. Small, wooden, leaves snaking in through gaps in the roof and dropping in tendril-like vines down the walls.

On the floor, in front of the fire, a sheepskin rug. Pale. Soft.

The door behind me clatters open. I move to one side, even though I know they cannot see me because, although this is real, it is not *now*.

"Kayan . . ." *Her* voice ripples through the air, teasing it into whispers that land on my skin and torture me. She is in front of the fire, wearing a burgundy dress that skims her hips and accentuates her waist.

Her hair is tied up, and my lips part hungrily with the

knowledge it will soon be hanging down around her porcelain shoulders.

The boy appears. Over a century old but still every bit a
boy in his demeanour. Floppy hair, eager grin. He pulls her
towards him and kisses her deeply. She melts into the kiss,
and sighs deeply.

Then, there it is, his hand going up to the back of her
neck, tugging her hair loose, and watching it cascade down
her back. He pauses, staring at her as though she is the
most precious thing he has ever encountered, a gem or a
jewel he wants desperately to caress but is scared of
breaking.

Studying them, it is clear she is the one with the power. She
bites her lower lip with a sinfully playful smile, then reaches
back and unlaces her dress.

Kayan stands back and watches her. The outline of his
cock is visible behind the fabric of his pants, but he doesn't
touch it. He just watches her.

Slowly, she peels her dress down over her shoulders. She is
wearing no underwear, and when she steps out of the dress
and casts it aside, her body is gloriously, completely,
exposed.

Firelight kisses the curve of her hips. She cups her breasts
for him, then slips one hand down to part her lips. Her
eyes widen as she begins to play with herself. Still, he
watches.

His wings flutter slowly, curling in the air. She kneels in
front of him, and opens her mouth. Stunned, the fool
simply stands there, until she teases him with a twerk of
her eyebrows and gestures for him to remove his pants.

When he thrusts his cock into her mouth, it is done with tenderness, and I can tell she could take it harder. *Wants* it harder.

She tries to encourage it, bracing her hands on his hips and pulling him deeper into her, but he stops, leans down, and kisses her instead.

Frustration bubbles inside me. He is treating her like a delicate flower, a precious and fragile creature. But she wants more than that. She *needs* more than that.

Slowly, he lies down beside her. He kisses her forehead and smooths the hair from her face, and although this may not be what she needs in order to propel her to the heights of pleasure she deserves, she seems suddenly and completely content.

He fucks her gently, lovingly. His tongue roams her body. His hands skim her perfect skin. But she is the fire. She is the one who nibbles the edges of his wings, grabs his wrists and holds them above his head while she plunges down onto him, takes him to the edge of pleasure, then stops.

As they approach their climax, I brace myself.

Not for her pleasure, but for his pain.

He is on top of her. Her legs are wrapped around him, one hand on her clit, one on his chest. Right above his heart. She stares into his eyes. Her lips part with a high-pitched moan. He moans too. They are moving in unison, playing to each other's rhythm. She tilts her head back, digs her fingernails into his chest. Moans louder.

He thumps the rug with his fist, next to her head. His body tenses. Her hand quickens, making harder and faster circles that pull deep coils of arousal from her core.

Her body shakes. Her wings glow. An orgasm washes over her, trickling through her body. He cries out, and she moans in response because she thinks it's a cry of release. When she realises it's not, she tries to push him off her, but a bright white light surges from beneath her palm, fusing her skin to his.

She tries to scramble away, free herself, free him, but she can't.

A blue light bursts from his body, emanating from every pore, consuming the oxygen around them until they're both struggling to breathe. His wings glow brighter too. Bluer and bluer until there is another, final, burst of light.

He collapses forward.

She lies beneath him, panting, trembling. She pulls her arm free, the contact broken, and pushes him away. He rolls onto his back.

His eyes are grey. She calls his name but he doesn't answer. She tries to help him up and, finally, gets him to stand. But he still isn't speaking. She grabs a blanket, wraps it around him, then pulls on her dress without fastening it.

"We're going to get you some help," she whispers. "Maura will know what to do."

Kayan does not reply.

As they stumble past me, I retreat into the shadows.

Before the door closes, I catch a glimpse of their wings. His, limp and pale. Almost translucent. And hers . . . still vibrant, and purple, and strong. But now tinged with the slightest hint of blue.

The blue shimmers, undulates beneath the surface, filling the gaps between her veins. Then it disappears.

And so does she.

Chapter Nine

ALANA

*T*he castle is quiet and cold – as if it exists in a different place entirely from the rest of the city. We are taken quickly through the courtyard, past the grand doors that must lead to the entrance hall, and down a series of dark passageways that seem to be leading us to the belly of the building.

At the rear, near the stables, where everything smells of hay and dampness, a large trapdoor is opened and we are ushered into a pitch-dark hole.

I stumble as I descend the spiral staircase, bracing myself on the icy stone wall for support because, although my wings are free, I daren't move them for fear a guard will think I am about to take flight.

The movement of climbing downwards makes my thigh burn. Kayan hears me wince and inhale sharply. "Are you all right?" he asks. "Are you injured?"

"I was hit in the raid." I reach down and rub my thigh, the

contact making my entire leg start to throb. "I didn't think it had broken the skin but it must have."

"Those arrows were poisoned," Kayan says, stumbling behind me as he's shoved roughly by a guard who tells him to keep moving.

"They were," I say, trying to keep my tone light and worry-free. "But I'm sure it'll be fine. Maybe they'll let me see a healer." I glance back over my shoulder and meet Kayan's eyes. "After all, Eldrion doesn't want his prize possessions to keel over, does he?"

Before Kayan can reply, we reach the bottom of the stair-case and emerge into what looks like a cellar. The ceiling is low, causing the taller males in the group to almost brush the tops of their heads and the ridge of their wings on its curved surface.

A guard stomps ahead, lighting torches, then stops in front of a large iron grate.

"You'll be held here until Lord Eldrion decides what to do with you," he says, pulling the door to the cell open and nodding at us to head inside.

A few others file in first, then Kayan, but before my feet can cross the threshold there is a hand on my arm squeezing me tightly. "All except you," he says, studying my face. "Lord Eldrion requested the redhead be taken some-where else."

Acid-tinged dread thickens on my tongue. I shake my head, try to think of something I can say to persuade him to let me stay with the others, but I am aware it is futile. The guard takes my elbow and roughly jerks me out of the way so he can seal everyone else inside their cell.

"You'll be brought water and food soon enough," he says.

Is that sympathy in his voice?

I search for his eyes but he keeps his face tilted away, so I cannot see his features properly. I am almost certain it is sympathy I detected. "Where are you taking me?" I ask as he marches me through a separate door and up a separate staircase.

We emerge in a brightness that makes me shield my eyes.

A large entrance way with a bright, glinting chandelier in its centre and a huge curved staircase at its rear. "This way." The guard approaches the stairs and waits for me to ascend them first. Following close behind, he says, "Just so you know, you're being watched. Even when you think you're not. So, don't try anything if you want to live through this."

Again, there's that softness in his voice.

"Is it possible to live through this?" I ask, turning to look down at him. "What does Eldrion intend to do with us?"

The guard hesitates a moment, then narrows his eyes, shoves past me, and strides loudly down the corridor at the top of the stairs. I follow, my heart beating harder and louder with every step, until we reach a large oak door with a butterfly engraved on it.

"Here." The guard raps on the door with his knuckles.

After a pause, it swings open and he shoves me inside. "I asked what Eldrion intends to do with us," I call, turning around in the hope of catching him before the door closes.

But it is too late.

He has gone, and I am alone.

At least, I think I'm alone until a flicker of movement in the corner of the room startles me. "Don't be alarmed." A young, dark-haired woman wearing a black smock and a white apron holds up her palms at me – like I'm a frightened animal about to run from her. "Lord Eldrion asked me to take care of you. You'll not come to any harm in here."

"Take care of me?" Indignation, disbelief, and rage swirl in my stomach. "He just *bought* me at auction and locked my people in a jail cell. And he wants you to take care of me?"

"I'm Briony." The woman extends her hand. When I shake it, she smiles. "I'll be your maid."

My forehead creases sharply into a frown. "Maid?" I laugh and shake my head. "I am a prisoner. Prisoners do not have maids."

Briony tilts her head from side to side. "Apparently," she says, "Lord Eldrion has decided that *you* do."

After handing me a glass of water and watching me drink it, Briony gestures to a large bathtub in the corner of the room and asks if I'd like her to run it for me. "While you soak, I'll lay out some clothes for you. I gathered what I could at such short notice."

Again, I cannot help laughing. Why would Lord Eldrion do this? Why would he bring me here only to give me a servant and a bubble bath?

I have barely formed the question in my mind when the answer comes to me. Panic grips my throat and drips down into my limbs; there can only be one reason Lord Eldrion would want my body cleansed and polished and ready for him.

I think of Rosalie being dragged away after the Gloomweaver extolled her virtues as a potential breeder. A carrier of Sunborne children.

My arms go to my waist, and I hug myself tightly. For, in this moment, I know exactly what Eldrion wants.

He intends to claim me.

He intends to make me his.

I WANT TO RESIST. I WANT TO REFUSE TO BATHE, CRAWL into bed, and sleep until this nightmare is over. But I also desperately want to feel clean again, and to remember what my skin was like when it was not caked in dirt and sweat and remnants of the stranger who I still cannot get out of my mind. I also need time to think.

"Very well, I'll bathe." I nod and flex my fingers inside my gloves.

Briony nods and sighs a little, as if she is relieved she doesn't have to try to persuade me.

"But I want to do so alone."

"Of course." She turns her back on me and heads for the tub, turning the taps so that steaming hot water runs into the basin.

Facing away from me, I can see that her wings are not like mine. They are small, almost like Kayan's – the way they became after the accident. Thin with visible, spidery veins and a muted grey tinge to them that indicates she has no elemental magic.

"You are Shadowkind?" I ask, stepping closer.

Briony swirls some lotion into the tub and looks up at me, sleeves rolled up as she tests the temperature of the water. "I am," she says. "All those in servitude to Eldrion's family are Shadowkind." She bites her lower lip. "At least, we were until now."

I swallow forcefully. "You think he wants to keep the Leaf-borne as his servants, too?"

"It is not my place to speak of such things." Briony worries the hem of her sleeve with her fingers. I glance at her arm, and notice a spider's web of scars that make my stomach clench. She pulls the sleeve down, then stops the taps. "Your bath is ready, ma'am."

"Please, don't." I take her elbow.

She looks at my hand, frowns a little at the golden glove, then pulls away.

"Call me Alana. I am not your superior."

Briony smiles gently. "All creatures are superior to the Shadowkind," she says gently. Then she tilts her head in the direction of what I assume is a dressing room. "I'll attend to your wardrobe while you soak. Let me know when you're finished."

I watch her wings closely as she leaves. They do not move the way mine do. Instead, they sit motionless on her back, no twitching or fluttering. They are just . . . there.

Before getting into the tub, I cross to the window and pull open the shutters. Warm air hits my face, in complete contrast to the cold that hangs over the castle. I brace my hands on the sill and lean out. Looking up, I can see the parapet where Eldrion's guards patrol with the arrows.

If I jumped and flew, would they truly shoot me down?

I turn my gaze towards the ground. My rooms are in a tower above the courtyard. Below, I can see the horses, and the trapdoor that leads to the cellar where the others are being kept.

My head spins with thoughts I can't pull into place. They don't seem to line up, or make sense. It is as if I am thinking in tongues. Amidst them all, thoughts of the stranger behind the falls still keep creeping in.

What happened to him? He was not a Gloomweaver, that much I'm certain of. He was fae, but from where? Not Leafborne. Perhaps an Oceandweller or a Mountainborne.

I grip the sill tighter, my fingers grating against the stone as I try to steady my breathing.

There are many things I should be thinking of at this moment, and the stranger in the red mask is not one of them.

Beneath my rough brown dress, my thigh aches. Perhaps the warm water will soothe it. Perhaps if I'm not in pain, I'll be able to think more clearly. For there has to be *some* advantage to me being up here instead of down there in the dungeon. There has to be something I can do from here that will help the others.

Removing my dress, lifting it over my head, I cross to the tub, then remove my gloves too and step in, hooking my long legs over the rim then sinking down into the water.

My hair floats around my shoulders, becoming damp at the ends, and I sigh as the warm water laps at my stomach, my breasts, my arms, the binders on my wrists.

I scoop some water into my hands and splash my face.

But my thigh still burns and, raising my leg out of the water, I can see it is angry and red. I want to ask Briony for help. I want to ask if she has any way of healing it, but I am not yet certain I can trust her. I vow to search her aura when she returns. If I do, I'll know whether she is earnest or whether she is a spy sent by Eldrion to watch over me and report my movements.

What if she reports my injury to Eldrion and I'm slammed back into the dungeon? Or given back to the traders?

It seems that, by being here in this tower, I have the chance – even if it is a tiny glimmer of a chance – to help my people escape. So, I will do what I can to ensure he keeps me here as long as possible.

Even if that means . . .

I swallow hard and screw my eyes closed. There is something about Eldrion that makes my skin ache with intrigue. Yet, knowing what I know of his cruelty, how could I ever find him anything but reprehensible?

If he intends to touch me, to use my body, to keep me here as his plaything, how do I let that happen without wanting to scream and claw out his eyes and tear holes in his wings with my teeth and my nails?

I pinch the bridge of my nose.

A jolt of nausea springs into my throat and I turn to the

side of the tub, releasing the meagre contents of my stomach onto the stone floor.

Immediately, Briony appears in the doorway and hurries over. "You are burning up," she whispers, brushing her palm across my forehead. "You are sick?"

I allow the gates of my mind to open and, even though a haze is descending on me, I search out her emotions.

"My lady?" She shakes her head, then corrects herself. "Alana . . . are you injured?"

I nod at her, suddenly unable to speak because my lips and mouth are so very dry. Her concern is palpable. It swims in her eyes and in the air around her.

She is sincere.

Thank the stars she is not an enemy.

"I was hit by a Gloomweaver's arrow," I whisper. "Please, don't tell anyone. If Eldrion knows I'm weak he might send me to the dungeon and I can't –" I inhale sharply as pain ricochets up and down my leg.

Briony's eyes are wide and worried. She grabs a towel and moves to help me out of the tub. "My gloves," I mutter. "I need my gloves. I shouldn't touch you."

She frowns at me but, without asking questions, nods. She hands me the gold gloves and I pull them shakily over my hands, then allow her to help me out.

It is ridiculous, really. I don't need to touch her in order to feel what she is feeling; I perfected the art of using just my mind many years ago. And I *know* deep in my soul that I won't do to another what I did to Kayan. At least, not like this. Not by accidentally brushing their skin with mine.

What happened with Kayan was the result of passion, and exhilaration, and a complete loss of control.

Part of me wondered, when I was with the stranger behind the falls, whether I might hurt him the same way. As my body exploded beneath his touch, I wondered whether it really was my hands that did the damage to Kayan or if it was *all* of me.

But he escaped unharmed.

So, perhaps my mother was right; my power is at its strongest in my fingertips.

When I am sitting on the edge of the bed, drinking from a large mug of water, Briony kneels in front of me and examines my wound. "Alana, I need to get you some medicine. Stay here. I'll be right back." She glances at the window, at the encroaching evening sky. "We have to make sure you're well enough for the banquet."

"Banquet?" I ask, my eyes fluttering as I lower myself back onto the bed. "What banquet?"

"Lord Eldrion has requested your presence this evening as his guest." She is at the door, turning the handle. "I'll explain. But first, medicine."

And then she is gone, and a key turns in the lock, and I am alone.

Chapter Ten

ALANA

I see his face. Except, it is not his face. It is his mask.

I see him looking up at me, and I feel his fingers inside me. My body warms under the heat of his gaze. Warmer, warmer, so warm I can hardly breathe.

The stranger in the mask grabs hold of my hips and pulls me towards him. I want to feel his tongue between my thighs, but instead I feel the cool, smooth texture of his mask and my pleasure begins to fade.

He stands. He grips my shoulders this time, but his grip becomes harder, stronger, more vicious. His nails dig into my skin. I try to pry his fingers away from me, but I cannot make him move. I try to scream, but no sound comes out.

He pushes me hard, slams me against the wall of the cave. But then we're not in a cave anymore, we're in the forest. And the forest is burning.

The heat is back. I writhe against it, murmuring.

"Alana . . ." A voice I recognise bleeds through the smoke and the screaming. "Drink this."

I feel something cold and wet on my lips. I open my mouth and swallow as someone holds my chin steady. Then everything goes dark again.

The next time I open my eyes, the heat is gone and I'm shivering. Briony is sitting at the end of the bed, her fingers laced together, shoulders hunched with worry. Her concern washes over me like waves of nausea.

"I'm all right," I whisper hoarsely, sitting up on the pillows. Somehow, I'm now in a robe instead of a towel. But my gloves are still on. She didn't remove them.

Smiling, Briony exhales loudly and holds her hand in front of her stomach. The relief she feels is palpable, and makes me feel a little lighter in response because *someone* here is concerned for me. Someone genuinely wants me to be okay.

"I'm sorry," she says, taking my elbow and helping me sit up. "But we don't have much time. The tincture I gave you isn't a fix, but it should treat your fever long enough for you to get through this evening. When you return tonight, I'll have our healer come and see you. Eldrion mustn't know. We aren't supposed to . . ." Briony trails off, shaking her head. "I'm saying too much," she tuts at herself. "For now, the most important thing is that you're expected at the banquet and we need to get you dressed."

Without really thinking, I swing my legs around and plant my feet on the fur rug beside the bed. I wriggle my toes into its softness and try to stop my head from spinning. Lifting the robe, I assess my thigh. Still red, but less angry and less painful.

"You'll feel a little lightheaded for the rest of the night." Briony has crossed the room. She disappears into the dressing room, then returns holding a long, black dress on a hanger. She lays it on the bed, then sets some underwear beside it; a corset that looks horribly uncomfortable and some lace panties.

"Do you need help?" she asks when I don't move.

I shake my head and rise shakily to my feet, retracting my wings so I can change. Turning away from her, I remove the robe, step into the panties, then fasten the corset as far as I can.

Taking the hint, Briony laces it the rest of the way for me, then steps back while I put on the dress. It is far more form fitting than anything I would usually wear. It clings to my hips and my stomach and, with the corset beneath, accentuates my breasts in a way I haven't seen before.

Briony smiles when I turn around. She fetches a brush from the dresser and tends to my hair, then steps aside while I unfurl my wings and stretch them wide.

The sensation releases some of the tension in my muscles, and I flex them several more times as Briony watches. "I love the purple," she says, tilting her head. "More of a violet, really."

She moves once again to the dresser and opens the top drawer. "Perhaps that's why he asked you to wear these instead of the gold." Holding out her hand, she nods at the object she's holding and a twinge of jealousy spikes in the air between us. Examining her dour uniform, I understand why. It seems awfully unfair that I am being given dresses and corsets and she is not permitted to wear such things.

I hold out my hand before I realise what she has in her grasp. When I do, I blink hard and swipe a nervous hand across my forehead.

Briony is offering me a pair of purple gloves.

My stomach twists violently, and another wave of heat washes over me. This time, not from the fever.

I take them from her, fingers trembling. Because I'd know these gloves anywhere. They are not just *any* pair of purple gloves. They are mine. The gloves I left in the bottom of my trunk, in my cabin, in the forest.

I hold them up to the light to be sure, and there it is – the burn mark on the left thumb. From the day I pulled chestnuts from the fire and they almost caught light. The day I begged my parents not to make me wear them anymore and my mother sobbed and my father told me I had no choice.

These are my gloves.

I slide them on. Staring at them, turning my hands over, transfixed, I mutter, "Eldrion gave you these?"

Briony nods. She is confused by my reaction. Confused and worried. "He insisted you wear them tonight with the dress." She steps closer and looks up at me. "Is everything all right, my lady?"

No.

Everything is not all right.

Somehow, Eldrion knew these were mine. Suddenly, the fabric feels rough and heavy against my skin. Because if Eldrion knew they were mine, that means he knew me before he bought me.

Chapter Eleven

ALANA

*T*he Grand Hall thrums with anticipation. Opulent shadows flicker in the candlelight, and it is all so different and so far away from the forests of the Leafborne that my soul feels like crying.

I am standing amongst a sea of Sunborne fae from the citadel. Gathered together like this, their magic is palpable. I felt it as I walked through the streets towards Eldrion's castle. But now they are pressed together, at least one hundred bodies filling the throne room with huge wings and even bigger egos, their strength so noticeable it brings beads of sweat to the back of my neck.

I always wondered why the Sunborne considered themselves so superior to other fae. Despite reading about arcane magic, and mind magic, and all the other kinds of magic the Sunborne possess, I still didn't fully understand.

Here, now, I do.

For – even with the gates of my empathy sealed tightly – I can tell that their magic is different from elemental magic.

It is stronger, and more dangerous, and it fights against the very air itself.

Leafborne fae might be able to *control* the air if they are so aligned, but there are Sunborne here who could extinguish the air completely. Who could make the universe implode if that is what they chose. It is a miracle they do not, and it makes me wonder what power Eldrion must possess that he is able to rule over them all the way he does.

At my side, Briony tugs on my sleeve. I glance at her, adjusting my gloves and trying not to let the significance of Eldrion's gift creep insidiously into my consciousness.

If he is playing games, I will not join in. I will not be manipulated.

"There will be a performance," Briony whispers. "Then the feast."

"How often does this happen?"

Briony shrugs. "Whenever Eldrion feels he has something to celebrate."

I wrap my arms around myself and rub my forearms. A shiver runs through me, and I have no idea whether it is because of the poison that still lurks in my veins or in anticipation of the night to come.

"He is not bringing the others to watch?" I ask, scanning the room even though I know I will not see any sign of a Leafborne in the crowd.

"No, only you." Briony looks away from me and nods towards the centre of the room.

Usually, when I am in a crowd, I am noticed, stared at,

backed away from. But at this moment, all eyes are drawn in the same direction. Waiting for the *entertainment* to begin.

"Why is Eldrion allowing me to walk free like this?" I whisper.

Briony simply shrugs. "He knows you can't escape," she says. "There are eyes on you. Always. Remember that."

Before I can reply, darkness descends further, then a spotlight appears.

A figure emerges. His bare feet caress the stone floor silently as he strides into view, positioning himself in the centre of the spotlight as if he is presenting himself for our appraisal.

He is tall and slender, with the physique of an athlete, not a fighter. Cords of muscle run in rivulets down his arms, and beneath a black leather mask, he wears charcoal around his dark brown eyes.

Those eyes . . . I feel the urge to move closer.

"That's Finn," Briony says. "Eldrion's favourite jester. His *only* jester since the others were . . ." She hesitates and glances at me. "Executed."

"Executed?" The word thickens on my tongue.

"They were no longer to his liking," Briony replies, hugging her waist as if she is very keenly aware that this could be her fate too if she displeases the man who owns her.

In front of us, the jester reaches up, grasping a length of black rope that dangles from the high ceiling. With a powerful leap, he swings himself upwards, his body twisting and contorting in mid-air as he climbs higher and higher.

The audience gasps as he performs a series of breathtaking aerial manoeuvres, his body spinning and flipping in ways that seem to defy the very laws of gravity. He wraps himself in the rope, using it as an extension of his own body, dancing through the air as if he is flying.

Except, his wings are small – painfully small, like Briony's – and he is not using them.

"He is Shadowkind, like you?" I ask her.

She nods solemnly. "We all are. All the servants."

The jester's aerial display lasts for several more impressive minutes, then he descends back to the ground. Breathing heavily, he splays his fingers and pushes out his chest.

He drops the rope and stands completely still, watching the crowd.

A drumbeat sounds from somewhere at the back of the room and the jester paces out of the spotlight. In time with the beat, he walks slowly around the inner circle of his audience like a tiger prowling in a cage.

A belt of silver chains encircles his waist and he wears leather pants but nothing on his torso. As he paces, I slip forward in the crowd. My breath swells, straining against my ribs; he is captivating. I cannot look away.

As I stare at him, the air around him darkens but, amongst this ocean of power, his lack of magic shines like a beacon.

Somehow, he feels pure. Different from anyone I've ever encountered before and, yet, familiar at the same time.

I watch him meet the eyes of every man and woman in the audience, not speaking, just staring into their souls. When he reaches me, my hand involuntarily goes to my stomach and my entire body fizzes with heat.

He lingers longer on me than any of the others. His eyes find mine and hold my gaze steady as waves of warmth drip down my spine.

I know those eyes.

Staring at me, he does not blink or move, just holds me there. Captured by the secret that swells between us. He inclines his head the smallest fraction. A movement so slight no one else would ever notice it.

I do the same.

Because I know exactly *how* I know him and where I last saw those eyes; I saw them looking down at me while he held me close and the falls thundered around us.

I know him because he fucked me, and because − for the first time in one hundred years − he reminded me what it was like to be wanted.

I want to drop my guard and feel him. I want to pull off my gloves and slam my hand against his skin and absorb every bit of him because he is so completely different to anyone I have felt before. I felt it then, and I feel it now − amplified by the strength of the Sunborne and by our surroundings.

The sensation is sudden and overwhelming, and I am almost certain I'm blushing.

But then he turns, and his wings appear. Paper thin and almost completely devoid of colour, there are places where the light shines right through them as if they are not even there, and the fibres that strengthen them are almost completely invisible.

They are more like the memory of a pair of wings. A whisper. An illusion.

When he turns and I see the piercings that puncture their delicate ridges, the heat in my belly turns to ice. I have never seen so many but I know what those piercings mean, and I know now why he kept his wings hidden from me in the forest.

Because if I'd seen them, I'd have known he was Shadowkind and I'd have asked him to explain why he was there. In our forest. At our festival.

He moves, and the piercings at the tops of his wings catch the light. I have read about them; there is one for every generation of his family that has been in servitude to the Luminael. And there are almost too many to count.

The ones at the very top chime gently as he returns to the spotlight, catching the eye of a woman with bright blue wings and silvery hair.

With deliberate grace, he beckons her forward. She grins and turns to her friends, who are nodding and smiling with approval. The jester – Finn, his name is Finn – holds out his hand and she accepts, a smirk playing on her lips.

Jealousy constricts in my throat.

He positions her in the centre of the light, then runs his hands down her arms and turns her palms up towards the ceiling. He reaches into his pocket and takes out a piece of thick, black rope. He presses it into her hands, then whispers something into her ear that causes her eyes to widen.

"What's happening?" I turn, looking for Briony, but she has disappeared amongst the swathe of unfamiliar faces.

The drums beat faster, and the jester begins to dance. He contorts his body to the beat, telling a story I can't interpret. Then – when the drums reach their crescendo – he stops, splays out his arms, and looks down at his feet. There is a moment of complete silence, and then he turns to face the woman and kneel at her feet.

The woman looks down at him and licks her lower lip. She assesses the ribbon in her hands, then pulls it taut.

The jester looks up at her and nods.

She smiles, then steps around him and – pressing all her weight onto his wings – pushes so they curl inward.

Finn lets out an anguished cry. The crowd claps and cheers. Beneath my skin, my own wings shudder with sympathy and I yearn to be closer to him.

When his wings are fully curled in, pressed against his back in an impossibly painful position, the jester raises his arms. Without hesitation, the woman begins to bind him. She snakes the rope around, and around, and around his body – pulling it tighter every time his wings twitch or he moans in discomfort.

This Sunborne fae revels in the control she's been granted and the audience watches with a mixture of fascination and arousal.

Gracefully, Finn stands. His wings are bound tightly, his movements deliberately restricted. This time, when he paces the circle, he keeps his back to us, allowing us to see the way the rope presses against the tissue-like flesh of his wings and how they visibly pulsate with pain.

I flex my fingers, ice-cold inside my gloves, and look away. I'm about to push back through the crowd when the air changes. The drums return – louder, faster, harder. The jester roars. His muscles strain, his eyes flash. And with a sudden, forceful motion, he breaks free from the bindings, his wings springing free.

A smile parts my lips but quickly fades when this moment – which in another place could signify a reclaiming of power – is met with laughter and applause. As if it is a hilarious joke.

The Sunborne view the jester's display of strength as simply part of the evening's entertainment. They clap, and laugh, and the Sunborne woman who bound his wings sashays back to her husband with a smirk on her face that makes me want to scream. Her husband squeezes her arm and kisses her cheek, staring at her as if her participation in the dance has affirmed her dominance rather than undermined it.

The jester stands completely still, breathing heavily, eyes closed. A strong jaw and a stubbled chin protrude from the mask he wears. His lips are full, and his hair protrudes in unruly tufts. His throat twitches when he locks his gaze on mine.

A shudder runs through me and settles beneath my skin, simmering, fizzing, vibrating. How is he here? What does it mean that we have been brought together like this?

The music changes. The drums are no longer sinister heartbeats but pulsing rhythms that nudge the Sunborne court into a flurry of movement.

As they filter towards the centre of the room and begin to dance, the jester remains amongst them. Now performing magic tricks, winking and smiling, his entire demeanour has changed. And I do not need to be feeling in order to see it.

With a flourish of his hands, he captures the attention of those nearest him. While some continue to dance, others form a small crowd around his slender figure. I linger on the periphery, entranced by the shift in his aura. It is as if he possesses two different faces, and it is impossible – even for me – to tell which is real.

Grinning at a pale-haired Sunborne male, the jester plucks a single leaf from the air – a leaf that wasn't there a moment ago. Vibrant green and seemingly ordinary, it twirls between his fingers. His lips begin to move and, with a whispered incantation that is barely audible above the murmur of the crowd, the leaf starts to shimmer, casting a soft, emerald glow around him.

Onlookers lean in as the jester, with a sly grin, folds the leaf in his palms. When he opens his hands again, the leaf has transformed into a fluttering butterfly, its pale, purple wings catching the light as it takes flight amongst the audience.

"Is that all?" A woman nearby coughs.

"Shadowkind have little magic," replies another. "What did you expect?"

"He should stick to dancing."

The other woman hums in agreement, and something snags in my gut when her eyes catch on the jester's muscled physique. Jealousy? Am I jealous that she is looking at him that way?

I'm still watching her, trying to interpret my own emotions – which somehow seems so much harder when I am blocking others' – when her eyes widen.

With a subtle flick of his wrist, the jester has directed the butterfly in a graceful arc over the heads of the onlookers. It flutters inches away from the woman who asked, *is that all?*

She stares at it, a pitying smirk on her face.

Then, in a blink, the single butterfly becomes two, four, ten, fifty . . . a cascading effect that continues until a small, mesmerising swarm of identical pale purple butterflies flutters up to fill the ceiling of the ballroom.

Each butterfly moves in perfect synchronisation, forming intricate patterns in the air – first the shape of a blooming flower, then shifting into the form of a dancing fae, and finally, a delicate, fluttering crown that seems to hover directly above the jester's head.

As he moves, the piercings on his wings chime gently and a smile parts my lips because my butterflies are always purple too.

As the butterflies dissolve back into harmless leaves, floating gently to the floor, a round of applause fills the room. The jester bows deeply, his eyes sparkling with mischief and the faintest hint of pride, before moving on to his next trick.

The dichotomy of his auras is enchanting. I cannot stop staring at him. While he is now full of jovial smiles and laughter, the first part of his act meant something. Deep in his soul.

And I wonder if it meant something to Briony and the other Shadowkind of Eldrion's court, or if that is why she walked away – because she couldn't bear to watch him.

For the audience, it was entertaining. For him, it was bigger than that. It was a fuck-you to the man who keeps him here.

A hand on my elbow forces me to turn away from him. Briony blinks up at me. Her face is pale, and she is worrying her lower lip with her teeth.

"What is it?" I ask, my brow crumpling into a frown.

She glances towards the empty throne at the helm of the hall. "Lord Eldrion requests your presence," she says, staring at her feet, swallowing hard. "In his chambers."

I cross my arms in front of my stomach, bringing my wings with them to cradle my shoulders. "I assume I cannot refuse?"

Briony shakes her head. "No, you may not."

"Very well." I draw myself up, determined to fight with every breath in my body rather than let this man lay a single finger on me – because that is clearly what he has planned. "Take me to him."

Chapter Twelve

ELDRION

*M*y chambers are dark, lit only by a series of flickering lanterns. I want it this way; I do not want her to see me too clearly. Not yet.

When she enters, she strides into the room like a queen. As if she expects me to fall at her feet.

I almost do.

For she is every bit as beautiful as I expected her to be.

Even when I saw her at that damned arena with dirt on her face, and tangled hair, wearing nothing but that hideous outfit they dressed her in, she was the most stunning creature I'd ever laid eyes on.

Like this – in the dress I gave her – she is even more resplendent. But she is also disarming.

"You summoned me," she says sharply, tapping her bare foot on the cold flagstone floor.

"I did."

"You bought me."

"I did."

"Why?" She cocks an eyebrow at me, and takes a step closer. If she is afraid of me, she is not showing it. But then, she doesn't know me yet.

She doesn't know what I'm capable of.

I am in shadow, seated in the large armchair by the window, drawn back in its embrace so the moon does not light my features. Slowly, I lean forward and steeple my fingers together. Behind me, my wings unfurl to their fullest, most impressive length.

Her eyes flicker, but she does not move away.

"I bought you because you will be useful to me." My gaze lands on her arms. Good, she is wearing the gloves.

I stand and close the space between us in one large stride.

She shudders as she looks up at me. Tall for a woman, but not nearly as tall as me, she pushes back her shoulders. She is trying to look powerful, but the gesture does nothing but accentuate her chest and make me want to grab hold of her waist.

She was not supposed to be this beautiful. My man told me she was; after the long months he spent following her, tracking her movements, he told me of her beauty and of the fire that lives in her belly. But I have known beautiful women before, and I did not expect *this*.

Now she stands before me, I understand why she is so important.

I just do not understand *how*.

Not yet.

"Have you settled into your chambers?" I ask, pacing around her as she stands stock-still, taking in the curve of her hips and the way her hair hangs down to the middle of her back.

"Why have you given me chambers?" she counters.

"I'm glad you found the dress I left you." I ignore her question and continue talking. "And the gloves." I stop in front of her, reach out, and tweak the index finger of the glove closest to me.

Alana Leafborne meets my eyes. Defiance swims in them. She breathes slowly and steadily and does not even flinch as I slowly tug the glove from her hand. "You know why I wear them," she says – a statement, not a question. "If you didn't, you wouldn't have gone to the effort of retrieving them and giving them back to me."

"An astute assessment." I look down at her hand. Pale and naked, it trembles a little and she clenches her fist, biting into her palm with her nails in an effort to stop it.

Slowly, very slowly, I reach out and wrap my hand around hers, engulfing her fist with my palm.

Her eyes widen. Her mouth opens a little and her entire body stiffens.

"You cannot hurt me," I growl.

"How can you be so sure?" she breathes.

I wait, holding her, staring into her eyes.

When nothing happens, a surge of frustration shakes my

wings and I stride away tutting. Turning back, I see her attempting to return the glove to her hand.

"No." I shake my head at her. "Leave it off. Both of them. When you are here, with me, you will not wear them."

I cross the room and snatch them from her and then, with a wave of my hand, I unfasten the binders on her wrists. "These neither."

As she rubs the red marks left by the cuffs, she stares at me, confusion etched on her porcelain face. "You're not worried I'll use my magic?"

"What magic do you have?" I ask, my lip curling. "You can read my thoughts, Alana, is that right?"

She does not look away from me as she says, "That's right."

"But the binders haven't prevented you from doing that."

I see the realisation wash over her. "No, they haven't," she says slowly.

"And you possess no other useful magic except the ability to cast incantations and enchantments? No elemental magic?"

She shakes her head.

"Then you will wear them outside of this room, to make those around you feel safe. But here, they will be removed the second you enter. Do you understand?"

For a long moment, she stares at her hands. Then she looks up at me. "I am to visit your chambers often?" she asks, tilting her head.

She thinks I intend to fuck her. She thinks that is what I brought her here for. Sadly, she is wrong. "Yes. Every day."

"Every day?" She presses her hands to her stomach and swallows hard.

"I wish to converse with you, Alana. Nothing more." I gesture to a chair by the fire. She frowns at me. "I wish to learn about you, and your people. I don't want anything else from you."

Tucking a loose strand of hair behind her ear, she shakes her head. "I don't understand."

"You are not a stupid woman. I think you do."

She frowns, then says, "Why me?"

I shrug and flop back into my chair. "Because you are nice to look at. And if I'm going to spend my days talking to someone, it will be someone pleasing to the eye."

"I'm sure there are many other–"

"I chose you!" My voice booms so loudly the lanterns rattle and the flames quiver.

Alana blinks at me.

"I chose you. Now, let us establish some rules."

She pinches the bridge of her nose as if she's trying to understand what I'm saying.

"Every evening, after supper, you will come here to me. You will wear whatever outfit I tell you to wear. You will answer my questions. And then you will return to your chambers. As long as you keep to this arrangement, no harm will come to you or your kin."

At the mention of her friends – even though they are friends who have exiled her for the past century – her eyes widen.

"They will be safe if you do as I say."

There is a long pause, then Alana dips her head and says, "Very well, my Llord. As you wish."

When she looks up, her eyes meet mine. Pale green, like sea glass, they are almost completely mesmerising. But as I look into them, I remember.

Light, and fire, and pain, and blood. Walls crumbling, waves lapping at the walls of the citadel. And the noise . . . the noise.

"That will be all for tonight." I stand up, walk to the window, and press my head against the glass. Outside, the citadel glows with moonlight and lanterns. The walls are intact. There is no noise.

"You swear they will be safe?" she repeats her question as she reaches the door.

"Do as I say, and they will not be harmed," I promise her.

She pauses. I can feel her breathing. I can feel the burning questions she needs to ask but daren't. Instead, she leaves silently. And I drink myself to sleep.

Chapter Thirteen

ALANA

*B*riony and I do not speak as we travel back through the castle towards my chambers. The Grand Hall still bustles with noise, but it is the noise of a feast, not a celebration, leading me to assume the jester's performance is over.

When we reach my chambers and the door closes behind us, I cross quickly to the bed and sit down hard. My breath rises in my chest, panic clawing at my insides because it took every ounce of willpower not to show weakness in front of that man.

"Are you all right, my lady?" Briony asks, kneeling in front of me, staring up.

I shake my head and motion for her to stand up. "Please stop calling me that. Call me Alana, and do not kneel for me," I tell her.

She nods, rubbing her arms nervously, then fetches me a glass of water because, clearly, she needs to feel like she's being helpful.

"What happened?" she asks. "Did he . . .?"

I drink down the water and push my hair back from my face. "We just talked," I tell her. I'm about to say he didn't lay a finger on me, but that's not entirely true.

I look down at my gloves. I pulled them back on as I left. And although I've worn them so many times before, they now feel unfamiliar and strange.

He did touch me, but it was not how I expected it to be. He is not how I expected him to be.

I stand up and cross to the window, opening it in the hope that a cool breeze might enter, then remembering the outside is nothing but thick, hot, and humid.

"He says he wants to see me every day." I turn, leaning against the sill and raising my eyebrows. "To talk."

Briony frowns at me quizzically. "He wants to talk with you?"

I nod and reach for another glass of water, wishing it was something stronger. "He said he wants to learn about the Leafborne – about the elementals. He said if I do what he asks and answer his questions, no harm will come to me or my people."

Briony has turned to sit down. She chooses the stone bench in front of the fireplace and leans forward onto her knees. "That is not what I expected," she says, and I can't quite read the look on her face.

Although I'm tempted to let down my guard and reach for her feelings, I don't. I feel like there is a friendship blossoming between us, and I have learned over the years that if my friendships are to be true, I must learn when it is appropriate to cross that boundary and enter their thoughts without their permission.

"Me neither," I reply. As I speak, my stomach growls loudly.

Briony stands, crosses to the dresser, takes the lid off a platter of bread and cheese and hands it to me. "I wasn't sure if you'd be attending the banquet, so I saved this for you," she says. "You should eat." Suddenly faced with food, I realise how hungry I am.

I eat while still standing, dropping crumbs down my dress and on the floor and not caring.

When I'm finished, Briony takes the plate away and fetches my robe from where it hangs on the back of the door. "Here," she says, "you should get changed. Finn will be here soon to look at your leg."

"Finn?" My heart skitters in my chest. "The jester?"

Briony tilts her head from side to side. "He is also a healer. Not that Lord Eldrion knows that. His aunt taught him before she died."

"Eldrion wouldn't allow him to practice if he knew?" I ask, trying to keep my face from betraying any hint of the fact I am *certain* I already know this man.

Briony makes a face. "Oh, no. Finn is here to entertain. And Eldrion doesn't like his Shadowkind forming bonds." She smiles a little, then shrugs. "You wonder why I'm such a chatterbox? It's because we're not allowed to speak to one another. If we're caught . . ."

"You're not allowed to *speak*?"

Shaking her head, Briony takes my dress and slings it over her arm. "Finn risks a lot by helping us. But he's good at going unnoticed in the shadows." She smooths the dress a little.

There is a fondness in her voice that hints at a sense of admiration for the man who danced in the air. The man who, I am certain, brought me to my knees with pleasure.

"He helps us not just with our bodies but with our minds. He has tinctures for anxiety and sadness. We experience a lot of both." She sighs a little. "He looks after us all. And he'll look after you," she says. "Now, change. I'll take this back to the kitchen and I'll give him the key. He won't come until after midnight, when the feast is over and everyone is sleeping."

Briony pauses at the door, turns, and meets my eyes. "Alana, Lord Eldrion must not find out that Finn has been here. He's doing this to help you. You must not betray him."

"I have no loyalty to Eldrion," I tell her. "I will give him only what little information I must in order to keep my people safe. But I promise you, Finn's secret is safe."

His name feels warm and pleasing on my tongue. *Finn*.

Briony nods, a smile twitching on her lips, then says, "I know this is probably extremely inappropriate. But, although I'm sorry for your situation, I'm also glad that you're here. It has been a long time since I had a friend."

She has closed the door and disappeared before I can think of how to reply. It has been a long time since I had a friend, too.

Perhaps there is some light in the darkness after all.

I<small>T IS PITCH-DARK OUTSIDE, AND THE MOON IS SHINING</small> brightly through the windows when I hear a key turn in my door. Still sitting in the chair by the fire, I turn towards the noise and brace myself.

The door opens slowly, a shadow creeping across the stone floor, snaking towards me.

When it closes again, I hold my breath. Someone is there, but I can't see him. I can only feel him. "Finn?"

When he appears, he is closer to me than I'd expected and a shudder shakes my shoulders.

"My lady," he says, echoing Briony's greeting and sweeping into a bow.

I stand, but stumble when pain shoots from my thigh to my pelvis. He reaches out and steadies me, glancing at the gloves I'm wearing, then helps me back into the chair. As he does, the bells on his wings chime gently and send shivers through my body.

"Please, call me Alana."

He nods, already kneeling in front of me. "As you wish."

Is he going to say something? Should I? Did I imagine the way we looked at each other when he was performing and caught my eye?

"Or should I call you Varia?" He looks up, his lips twitching with a smile that makes me grin.

"It *is* you." I reach out to touch him but he flinches and I stop. "I'm sorry —"

"Don't be sorry." He shakes his head, then catches my hand and presses it to the side of his face. "I just didn't expect to see you again."

"Are you sorry?" I ask.

He smiles again, and squeezes my gloved fingers. "No, I am happy. But that makes me sorry. Because I should not be happy that you are here."

"Briony said the same thing." I stroke his forehead and he leans into my touch.

"Did she sneak away from the castle to attend the forest centennial, too?" he asks, chuckling.

"No." I shake my head and ease back in my chair, allowing him to lift my leg onto his knee. "But I think she has been lonely."

Finn's smile drops a little. He presses his lips together, then says, "Loneliness is the Shadowkind's second biggest curse."

"What is your first?" I ask.

But he doesn't answer.

Wearing loose black pants and a brown jacket, open at the chest, a bag is slung across his chest. He opens it and begins to rummage around inside.

"You are still wearing a mask." I dip my head to meet his eyes. "Am I never to see your face?"

When he looks up, a smile curls his lip and dimples his jawline. "I am not permitted to remove it," he says. "But my face is not worth seeing, *si'thari*, trust me." He smiles again. "Yours, on the other hand."

I inhale slowly, wisps of pleasure settling on my skin.

"May I take a look?" he asks, fingers hovering above the opening crease of my robe.

I'm about to part my thighs for him when I realise he is talking about my injury and not something else. Gingerly, I lift the hem.

He does not look down until I have raised it high enough to expose the wound, just keeps his eyes trained on mine. And, somehow, the eye contact makes me feel more vulnerable than I would if he *was* staring at my naked flesh.

For it is as if he sees me.

"What happened?" he asks. "Briony wasn't sure."

"We were raided by Gloomweavers. They took us all. Whatever was in their arrows killed those who were struck in the heart." I pause, then quietly add, "What happened to you? Where did you go?"

Finn adjusts his mask at his ear and shakes his head. "I fled," he says. "I was afraid of being caught." He swallows forcefully and the muscles in his shoulders twitch. "I'm sorry," he mutters. "I should have stayed. Should have tried to help."

I reach out and slip my hand into his. "Don't be sorry." I squeeze gently, showing him I mean it. "I'm just very glad you're here now."

For a long moment, we simply stare at each other. Then Finn returns his attention to my leg. "Lucky for you, you were only grazed," he says. "Also lucky for you . . . Gloomweavers' potions are strong but easy to treat.

They're incredibly stupid. Haven't changed the ingredients in centuries."

I wince as he presses his fingertips to the sore, red flesh around the wound. "It's not infected," he says. "But I'll give you something topical for the wound itself and something to drink just to make sure it doesn't *become* infected."

I nod, flexing my foot because my ankle is at a strange angle and starting to ache.

As if he can tell, he lowers my leg to the ground. I am sad to lose contact, and my skin feels strangely cold without him beneath it.

As he prepares the remedies for my wounds, I take a deep breath and try to fight the urge to sleep. It feels like so long since I last slept.

Finn smiles at me. The crackling fire casts dancing shadows across his mask and accentuates his chiselled jaw. I find myself unable to tear my gaze away.

"I saw your performance for the court," I say, my voice barely above a whisper. "The way you moved . . . it must have taken many, many years to become so skillful."

Finn pauses, meeting my eyes. "I have been in Eldrion's keep for a long time," he says, giving his wings a small flutter that makes his tip-piercings chime.

I try to count how many others there are, lining the outer rim of each wing, but he answers for me. "Thirty," he says. "Thirty generations of my lineage have been indentured to Eldrion's family."

"Thirty?" I breathe out heavily. That's *thousands* of years.

"You enjoyed the dance?" he asks, smoothing some dark grey lotion onto his fingers, then bringing them to my thigh.

"Enjoyed?" I bite my lower lip as his fingertips meet my skin. "I found it harrowing, actually."

A wry smile parts his lips. "You'd be the only one," he says. "I perform that dance every time Eldrion asks me to entertain the citadel. Every time, I think maybe *this* will be the time they realise what they're witnessing. They never do." He pauses, frowns, and looks up at me with his deep brown eyes. "Or maybe they do and that's why they enjoy it. I wouldn't put anything past a Sunborne."

"Explain it to me." I lean forward as he caresses my wound. The lotion has already soaked in, and yet he is still making slow circles with his fingers. "I understood it was about your servitude. But I feel as though there's more than I could see . . ."

Finn sits back on his heels, slowly removing his hand. He passes me a vial of something blue and gestures for me to drink it.

I swallow it down quickly, wincing as it burns my throat.

"The dance is a reflection of my people's history. How much do you know about Shadowkind fae?"

I tuck my hair behind my ear. "Shamefully little," I reply. "There isn't much in our history books."

"Of course, there isn't." Finn chuckles. "Well, the Shadowkind have been in captivity for thousands of years."

I glance at his piercings, my stomach tightening.

"When the Sunborne first started using us for labour, they began to bind our wings."

"Bind them?" I swallow hard, trying to force the words down the sudden thickness of my throat.

Finn nods and adjusts his mask. Behind it, his eyes are rimmed with charcoal. "And still today," he says. "When a Shadowkind is born, their wings are bound to their body. While Leafborne and Sunborne have magic deep inside, ours is inside our wings. By binding them, preventing them from growing, we are stripped of our magic."

Cold, lingering disgust snakes down my spine. "How did I not know this?" I breathe.

"Few people do, and even those who do pretend they don't." Finn places a hand on my bare knee, and squeezes. "Don't feel bad, Alana."

I hold my breath, acutely aware of the rise and fall of Finn's chest, the sound of his breathing mingling with the crackle of the flames in the grate of the fire.

"I'm an empath," I laugh. "Feeling bad for others is what I do."

"But you're shielding right now?" he says, raising his eyebrows at me.

"How do you know?"

"I've known empaths before," he says. "Not many. But a few."

I stifle a yawn, and Finn smiles at me. "I want to keep talking to you."

"You should rest." He slips his arms beneath me and lifts me from the chair. I allow myself to brush his lips with my thumb.

But he does not kiss me. Instead, he lowers me onto the bed and tucks me beneath the sheets. He is at the door when he says, "What happened behind the falls cannot happen again, Alana."

I sit up, searching for him in the shadows.

But once again, he is gone.

Chapter Fourteen

FINN

*S*eeing *her* face in the crowd of Sunborne was like seeing the brightest, most beautiful jewel in the world and realising it had been stolen. Caged. Contained.

It took every ounce of strength I had not to stride over and take her in my arms and whisk her up into the air, high above those aristocratic fuckers.

But I couldn't. Because I cannot do anything without Eldrion's permission.

The one rebellion I have is the binding display at the start of my act. When I first performed it, I almost *hoped* he would punish me for it. I hoped it would cause him so much humiliation – to be faced with his family's worst crimes – that he would beat me for days.

He did not beat me. Instead, he laughed.

He laughed, and then everyone else laughed, and – just like that – it became part of the act. Titillation for the noble women of the citadel who feel pretty and powerful when they wrap the bindings around my torso.

The fact I break free means nothing to them.

But it meant something to her. She saw it. And I see in her what I saw in the forest; the spark of someone who *knows* what it is to be different but who doesn't know she has the power to make things better.

I might be trapped beneath Eldrion's wing. But *she* has something I don't; she has magic. And if she plays this the right way, she might just be able to help us all.

"Finn?" Briony steps out of the door to the servants' dorm and presses her back against the wall. Silently, I move into the shadows beside her.

While she shares with ten other women, I at least have the privilege of my own chambers and I am desperate to return to them now.

As always, performing has left me exhausted. But being so close to Alana has left me with other feelings, too. Ones I need to be alone to deal with.

"How is she?" Briony bites her lower lip. She is one of the younger Shadowkind servants, just fifty-two years old but with already sallow skin and dark hair that no longer shines.

Her bindings were removed last year. Since then, they have yet to move. At least mine have remembered that over the years.

"She'll be fine," I tell her, adjusting my bag of supplies on my shoulder. "I must go now."

"Wait." She takes my elbow, blushes, then lets go of it. I have never fucked her, but she has always wanted me to and tonight is no different.

"I have to go, Briony." I move to walk away, because I have absolutely no interest in lying with her tonight or any other night, but she shakes her head.

"Please, wait. The Leafborne in the dungeon. Some of them need help."

Under any other circumstances, I'd refuse Briony's request. Getting from my chambers to the dungeons is a risk I'd rarely take, let alone at this time of night – too close to sunrise for my liking. But my treacherous conscience asks me what Alana would say if she knew I'd refused to help her kin, and I find myself saying, "Very well."

We leave the castle through the servants' entrance and cross the courtyard to the trapdoor that leads to the dungeon. It creaks when we pull it open, but instead of hesitating I jump swiftly down inside and bring Briony with me.

"Are they not guarded?" I hiss as we approach the door that will lead to the cells.

"Yes, but it is Henrik on duty tonight. He will let us in."

I press my lips together. Henrik and I have never been on good terms. Something about me unnerves him, and the way he looks at me makes me want to curl my fist and punch him in his broad, ugly nose.

I make a *hrmph* sound, but Briony doesn't respond.

True to her word, however, Henrik opens the door when we tap on it and ushers us inside. At the back of the low-ceilinged stone dungeon is a large cell. Bars reach from the floor to the ceiling and stretch across the width of the room. Inside, I count twenty-one Leafborne fae. All in chains.

Some are sleeping, their heads lolling uncomfortably. Others are whispering in the darkness.

When I approach, they start to stir and nudge each other and stare at me with wide, frightened eyes. I hold out my palms to them. "I'm a friend," I say gently. "Here to help. I heard some of you are injured?"

For a long moment, no one replies. But then a fae with blond curly hair and surprisingly skinny wings drags himself to his feet and says, "Are you able to get into the cell?"

I glance over my shoulder at Henrik, who swallows hard, then shakes his head. "I can't. It's one thing letting you down here. If they escaped . . ."

I turn back to the blond fae. "I'm afraid not. Tell me what ails you, and I'll pass what remedies I have through the bars."

"I am not hurt," he replies. "But my friend Talia has glass in her foot, and Ben thinks he has broken his wrist."

I start with Talia. She lifts her foot, and I squint into the dark to examine it. Somehow, I manage to instruct her to pull the glass free, then pass antiseptic and bandages through the bars. They are handed along the line of chained-up fae, and the woman next to her helps her wrap her foot.

"You'll have to remove the bandage by morning," I tell her. "If it's seen . . ."

She nods at me, sighing with relief now the pain is subsiding. "Thank you," she says. "I promise I'll hide it."

Next, the man with the broken wrist. Altogether more difficult to treat without being able to touch it. I instruct the blond fae, who tells me his name is Kayan, to examine it for me and pinch the bridge of my nose as I try to figure out how exactly I'm going to splint this man's wrist without it being seen.

Deciding there is no way to do this, I gesture to the pants he's wearing. "You'll need to tear a strip from your pants and make a sling. I can give you something for the pain, but it should look as though you made the sling yourself."

Kayan, the blond, looks like he's about to protest but when I give him a withering stare, he stops.

I wait until Ben has finished with the sling, then pat the iron bars and say, "I must go now, good night and good luck."

"Sir . . ." Kayan speaks loudly – too loudly – and prompts a 'hush' from Henrik.

I cock an eyebrow at him; no one has ever called me *sir* before.

"Please, tell us, is there any chance we will escape here?"

Laughing a little, I allow the bells on my wing tips to chime; one thing Eldrion doesn't know about me is that I've perfected the art of keeping them completely still, and silent, when I don't want to be heard. I am about to tell him there is no chance when something makes me say, "Ordinarily, to others in your position, I'd say no." I bite the inside of my cheek. "But your Alana is an impressive woman, and Eldrion seems to have taken a liking to her. If anyone is in a position to help you, it's her."

"Alana?" Kayan's eyes brighten, and an unexpected twinge of jealousy tugs my gut. "You've seen Alana?"

"I have," I reply firmly. "Eldrion has given her chambers in the castle."

"Is she all right?"

From somewhere at the back of the cell, someone sneers, "Don't waste your energy being concerned for her, Kayan. As usual, she is looking after herself."

Whoever spoke, I cannot see them. But I am gripped by the overwhelming urge to throw open the cell door, seek them out, and choke an apology from their miserable lips.

"She is concerned for you all, and frightened, but she is safe for now." I narrow my eyes at Kayan, trying to discern what he and Alana are to one another. It is only when he shifts, trying to lean closer to me, that I notice his wings.

They are surprisingly thin – not unlike mine. Very unlike any other Leafborne I've encountered.

"I will tell her you asked after her when I see her next." I nod at him.

"Bring her to see us." Kayan looks from me to Briony, who is standing silently beside Henrik. "Please. Bring her here, so we can see she is all right."

"It seems not all of you care whether she is *all right*." My jaw twitches with irritation as the rest of the cell quiets.

"I care." Kayan pushes back his shoulders, puffing out his chest as much as he can from the confines of his restraints.

I tilt my head to one side and sigh. "I won't be visiting you again. I wish you luck." Then I turn to Henrik and say, "Goodnight, friend," patting him hard on the shoulder.

Glaring at me, he pulls open the dungeon door. On her way out, he grabs Briony by the waist and whispers something into her ear. She gives him a sultry smile, nods, and follows me back up into the courtyard.

I am back in my chamber when it occurs to me that perhaps I should let Alana decide whether she wants to see her people or not.

Who am I to make that decision for her?

Who am I to take yet another choice away from her?

As I drift into a fitful sleep, I vow that next time I see her, I will give her that choice. I will let her take control of what little she can because I understand what it is like to live in Eldrion's gilded prison.

While she is here, I will do what I can to comfort her.

I will be what she needs when she needs it.

Because, in two hundred and fifty years, no one has ever granted me that grace. And I would risk Eldrion's wrath to give her what she needs.

Chapter Fifteen

KAYAN

*R*awk's foot sticks out from beneath a pile of used grain sacks that were brought down to the dungeon in the early hours of the morning. The guard huffed something about this not being a storage facility, glanced at us, then added, "Not that kind, anyway."

But the one transporting the used sacks simply shrugged and insisted.

Eventually, after a standoff in which they just stared at one another for several long minutes, the guard huffed that they could be dumped in the corner. The one carrying the sacks shuffled over, looked down at Rawk's greying body and snapped, "What are you doing with this guy?"

"Don't know," the guard shrugged. "Maybe he'll go to recycling with the sacks."

The sack-carrier laughed, the shared joke at Rawk's lifeless expense breaking the tension between them. Then he ditched them on top of Rawk's body, shook the guard's hand, agreed to meet for a game of dice later, and left.

I feel the need to move the sacks from his face or to hide his feet, so he is either completely buried or free to breathe. I know he can't breathe. I know he'll never breathe again, but it feels unbelievable to me that someone so full of life – and arrogance – a few days ago is now gone. Extinguished.

"You could have been an elder before him, you know." Maura nudges my elbow. She has followed my line of sight and is staring at Rawk's feet too.

"I don't think I'd ever have been an elder, Maura, even if I had kept my magic." As I speak, my wings flutter involuntarily.

Turning her grey eyes on me, Maura sighs heavily. "You were born to be an elder, Kayan. I knew it from the moment I saw you." Her lips twitch into a smile. "I delivered you, you know."

"I do know," I reply warmly.

She reaches for my hand and squeezes it. The motion causes her chains to grate and she sighs heavily. "I am sorry she took away your chance."

She is talking about Alana. While others in the village have grown to tolerate her over the years, Maura has actively campaigned for Alana's expulsion from the Leafborne many times. Empathy is not an elemental ability. She should not have been amongst us in the first place, was her most commonly used argument.

But despite everything, even though Alana wasn't speaking to me – hasn't spoken to me for an entire century – I couldn't bring myself to agree.

"What happened was an accident." I wrap my fingers around my chain and use it to steady myself because my legs are starting to feel weak from hunger. "She didn't intend to hurt me, Maura. She'd been trying to learn to control her powers. She has greater control over them now."

Maura tuts loudly and jerks her head away. She doesn't want to hear me making excuses for Alana. Without turning back towards me, changing the subject, she says brusquely, "What about Rosalie?"

A knot forms in my throat. "Rosalie . . ."

"You two were close to becoming betrothed, I believe." Maura lowers herself to the floor and leans back against the wall. Around us, the others are starting to shuffle and murmur as they wake up. Even though there is no daylight present.

I scrape my fingers through my hair and try not to picture her being dragged away from me. A knot tightens in my throat. "Yes, and we still will be."

Maura looks up at me but doesn't speak. She doesn't need to. Her skin is smooth and almost completely free of wrinkles, her long, bright white hair the only true betrayal of her age. "Kayan . . ." She tilts her head. Sorrow and sympathy swim in her eyes.

"When we leave this place, I will find her." I inhale slowly, trying to encourage the air into my lungs in the hope it will ease the anxiety that has lodged itself below my ribcage.

Slowly, I sit down next to Maura. In the far corner of the cells, a few of the younger fae begin to pace back and forth. Chained to the wall, they cannot go far and simply make slow, sad circles, their bare feet tapping silently against the cold stone floor.

The earth fae with the red hair, who looks like a willowier version of Alana, begins to cough. Her boyfriend, Pen, asks for water but the guard ignores him.

I look away, thoughts of Alana tugging incessantly at my mind.

"Where do you think Eldrion took her?" I mutter darkly.

Maura frowns at me. "Rosalie was bought before Eldrion —" she stops, sighs, and shakes her head. "You are talking about Alana."

"Do you think he intends to . . .?" I can't finish my sentence. Daren't say out loud what I've been thinking about all night. Over and over.

"I don't much care what he intends to do." Maura wraps her arms around her waist.

"That's not true," I reply firmly. "You dislike her, but you wouldn't wish harm on her."

I expect Maura to tell me I'm right, and laugh. But she doesn't. She just meets my eyes and, stoically, says, "You underestimate my hatred of the woman who broke you, Kayan."

THE DOOR TO THE DUNGEON CREAKS OPEN, CAUSING THE guard to leap up from his chair.

"Henrik . . ." A petite, dark-haired fae with small wings offers the guard a large smile. She is blushing.

"Briony." Henrik grins back, adjusting his belt in a way that makes me shudder a little. Not because he is an unattractive person, but because he is an unattractive soul. He has shown no care for us, no interest, no acknowledgement that we are anything other than ants to be squashed.

"I brought rations." Briony offers up a hessian sack, tied with string, and a flask of what looks like water.

Henrik takes them and strides over to us. Taking a large iron baton from his belt, he bangs the bars unnecessarily loudly. "Wake up, sleepy heads," he barks.

"I don't think anyone was sleeping," I reply, moving into his field of vision.

He narrows his eyes at me, then shoves an arm through the bars, offering me the sack. "Hand these out." He follows by giving me the water, too.

"This is all?" I ask, weighing the sack up and down in my hand. "For twenty of us?"

Henrik pauses, his eyebrows almost touching his hairline as his eyes widen. "Shall I take it back?" He moves to open the cell door.

"No, no, thank you," I force myself to say through gritted teeth. "We are grateful for your . . . hospitality."

As the others stand and watch, I open the sack and peer inside. "Bread," I say bluntly. "But not much of it." I stoop down and tip it onto the floor, then Maura helps me divide it into twenty minuscule portions while the water is passed around with the instruction to drink only a little until everyone has had a sip.

We eat our bread in silence. Mine hasn't touched my lips yet when my eyes land on Raine. With dark skin and dark hair, she is a powerful fire fae. She is also pregnant. I call her name and hold out my ration. She is within touching distance, and after hesitating, nods in quiet gratitude and accepts my offering.

"What's up with your wings?" Henrik's voice drifts over from where he is standing, sipping coffee, watching us. "They don't look like the rest." He jerks his head at the other Leafborne.

My jaw twitches. I do not owe this man an explanation.

"The woman your lord took up to his castle, that's what happened." Maura, however, answers for me. "She destroyed him. Took his powers. Drained him of his magic, and his senses. Took him years to even speak like himself again."

"Maura . . ." I warn. "Please."

Henrik's eyes widen a little. He rubs his chin, then glances at Briony, who is sitting by his desk with her own mug of coffee. I can't read the expression on her face, but something tells me this information means something to her.

"Is that so?" Henrik shakes his head. "Well, well. She sounds special, indeed."

I flex my wings. They ache with the sudden need to stretch wide and be free.

"She took your magic?"

"She didn't take it. It doesn't belong to her. It's just . . ." I trail off. I shouldn't be telling this man anything, but somehow I cannot help coming to Alana's defence.

Taking a moment to steady my breathing, I move as close to the bars as I can, and fix my gaze on Henrik. "My wings aren't dissimilar to yours."

His expression doesn't change but, behind him, Briony's wings twitch uncomfortably.

"You're Shadowkind?" I give a jerky nod, taking in his withered wings and the sallow tint to his skin. "Which means Eldrion owns you."

Henrik's fingers tighten on his coffee.

"Does he treat you well?"

"Quiet," Henrik mutters, rolling his eyes. But everything about his demeanour tells me I'm unnerving him.

"Have you never thought about escaping? Surely, there's nothing stopping you?" I frown at him, then gesture to the door. "You could walk out right now. You're not in chains. So, why are you here?"

"We can't leave." Briony stands up and strides past Henrik. Her eyes are wide, and she is clasping her mug tightly between her thin fingers. "He owns us. Do you know what that means?"

"From where I'm sitting it means you're cowards." I square my shoulders and look her straight in the face.

Henrik moves to her side. "We are no cowards," he growls.

"Kayan, enough." Maura nudges me. "Don't provoke them. It won't help."

"I'm not provoking them. I'm trying to understand why they're here. I always thought the Shadowkind were enslaved. Beaten. Badly treated." I shrug. "Looks like a pretty nice setup from where I'm sitting. All you have to do is abuse some prisoners, and –"

A sharp bolt of blinding pain ricochets through my knuckles. I'd been holding the bars, and fall back as Henrik lowers his iron baton. The mark it has left on my hand blazes red and angry.

Henrik is visibly shaking. "You have no idea," he spits.

Briony puts her hand on his shoulder. She whispers something to him and pulls him away. At the back of the room, she kisses him gently, and they continue to talk for a few more minutes. Then she squeezes his hand and leaves.

"Why did you do that?" Maura hisses as she examines my hand. "Why prod him like that? Why anger him? Are you trying to get yourself killed?"

"Because I needed to see how loyal they are to their lord." I meet her eyes, and lean in close. "And I got my answer . . . They hate him as much as we do. Which means we have a chance of getting them to help us escape."

Chapter Sixteen

ALANA

*HREE DAYS LATER*

For the past three days, I have seen Eldrion after supper.

For three days, the court has been filled with Sunborne watching Finn perform, and Briony tells me this is unusual. Normally, these kinds of celebrations happen sparingly. But it seems Eldrion feels the need to show off.

Briony thinks this means he is hiding something, that something is going on which he doesn't want the other Sunborne to know about, that he is using these nightly festivities to distract them.

If that's true, it seems to be working. Because every night they pour into the Grand Hall and they watch Finn perform, and they drink and dance and eat and fuck and go home, hedonistically sated.

It surprises me that Eldrion never joins the celebrations, yet his presence still feels palpable somehow. As if he is watching us even though he is not there.

Briony is always the one who takes me to him, and she always waits outside the door until we have finished talking. So far, for three consecutive nights, we have talked until sunrise.

He paces the room and asks me questions about the Leafborne's abilities, about when they first manifest, and how long it takes us to learn to control them. He asks about the colour of our wings and what it means. He asks whether the Leafborne are more in tune with the earth than the Mountain fae or the Ocean fae, and I tell him it doesn't work like that. "Although we are fae of the forest, our clan is still made up of many different affinities – water, air, earth, fire."

"But not you." Last night, after I had finished explaining for perhaps the hundredth time, he looked up at me from his armchair by the fire and steepled his fingers together.

I said nothing. Just met his eyes, waiting to see exactly how much he knew about me. Because we had still not discussed my gloves, or how he found them, or how much he knew of me before he brought me here.

"You have no affinity. You have mind magic." When he said that, I frowned.

Mind magic is powerful. Mind magic is something only the Sunborne possess and I am no Sunborne.

"Empathy is not mind magic," I replied eventually. "But you should know that. You should know all of this. You do not need a two-hundred-year-old Leafborne to tell you the things I am telling you."

In the shadow of the chair, Eldrion puffed out his wings, impressively wide, studying me carefully. "Who told you empathy is not mind magic?" he asked.

I looped back through my memories. Two hundred years; there are a lot of them. "My parents told me. The elders of my village told me. Our history books . . ." I pause and narrow my eyes, visualising the books I pored over when I was younger and trying to understand what it was that made me so different from the others.

Eldrion quirks an eyebrow at me. Everything about him is sharp, angular, fierce. His features are chiselled. Even his hair is poker straight, and his wings point like daggers at their tips in a way I haven't seen before.

"Our books talk little of empaths," I murmur, lacing my fingers together behind my back and feeling the strain of the corset beneath my dress.

"Every fae you've ever met has lied to you," he said brusquely, rising from his chair and stepping into the dim light so I could see the contours of his face and the dazzling brightness of his eyes. Towering over me.

That was last night.

But he did not give me a chance to ask what he meant, simply turned away, clicked his fingers, and told me we were done and that he would see me the next day.

Now, it is the next day and things have happened differently.

I am dressed for dinner, ready to spend the next hour torturously close to Finn but unable to touch him or talk to him, communicating with him only through stolen glances and longing, when Briony tells me Eldrion has requested my presence now.

My heart drops down into my stomach, partly because I am so disappointed I will not see Finn and partly because the change to our routine is unnerving.

"He says you needn't dress for dinner. He says you should wear outdoor clothes," Briony says, striding over to the wardrobe and starting to rustle amongst my things.

I call them my things but they are not my things. They're the things he gave me.

"Here," she says, pulling out a pair of dark jodhpurs and a grey knitted sweater. "The weather has turned. It's cold outside."

I put them on, finishing the outfit with a pair of large boots that make my feet incredibly uncomfortable. Briony too seems nervous, and I wonder whether she knows something that I don't.

We're at the door when she says, "Have you ever tried —" she stops mid-sentence and shakes her head.

"Tried what?" I ask, meeting her eyes.

She blinks up at me and worries her lower lip with her teeth. "Have you ever tried to feel what Eldrion is feeling?"

I hold my breath for a moment. Even though I trust Briony completely, my instinct is always to hold back when she asks me a question. Despite myself, I answer her truthfully. "No, I haven't. Why?"

She asks, now intrigued, "Not even to help? If you could tell whether he thought fondly of you or —" she pauses, searching for the word, and settles on saying, "or not?"

"Perhaps." I nod. "But I know nothing of his magic. And I know nothing of what he truly wants from me."

Leaning back against the doorframe so it must remain sharp for a moment longer, I fold my arms in front of my stomach and say, "Let's face it. He didn't bring me all the way here just to ask me questions about elementals. He is the oldest fae in the kingdom. He knows all there is to know about our magic, which means he wants me for something else. At first I thought it was sex. But that doesn't seem to be true, either. So, what does he want?"

"You think he wants your magic?"

"I don't know. We only started talking about it yesterday. It was the first time he'd mentioned my empathy, and what it means, and how it relates to me being a Leafborne, but he seemed to stop himself before he said too much."

I pause, trying desperately to articulate the thoughts that have been swirling in my mind for the past three days.

"Something became clear, though. Even here, in Luminael, empaths are a rarity."

"You didn't know that?" Briony asks, tilting her head at me.

"No," I reply, almost embarrassed by my own lack of awareness. "I didn't. I just always assumed there were more like me somewhere out here."

"Trust me," Briony says. "There are not."

I pinch the bridge of my nose and sigh. Something deep inside is telling me I shouldn't give Eldrion the opportunity to reach my magic, and that means keeping the gates up. It means continuing to go in blind and not being able to tell what he's thinking. But right now, I feel like that's the only way to keep myself safe. At least until I have figured out why he is so interested in me.

Why he stole my gloves and how he knew of me before I knew of him.

I smile a little and shake my head because I'm not even making very much sense to myself. But Briony seems to understand.

"Eldrion is powerful," she says. "More than powerful. You cannot trust anything he says. And no matter how he appears to you, you must remember that he has done unspeakable things." Her fingers go to her arm and the scars that I've seen several times before but have never asked about. "He's an evil person, Alana. Whatever he wants you for –" she reaches out and squeezes my upper arm. "Keep your guard up. That's what I'm saying. Do what you can to protect yourself and don't let him near your magic."

Chapter Seventeen

ALANA

*B*riony's words echo in my mind as I make my way to Eldrion's chambers, my heart pounding in my chest. The hallway stretches before me, dimly lit by flickering candles, and I can't help but feel a sense of unease wash over me.

As I round the corner, I nearly collide with Eldrion himself. He's dressed in a black cloak and riding boots, his dark hair swept back from his angular face. His eyes, piercing and intense, rake over my body, lingering on my hips for a moment too long.

"Come with me to the stables," he commands, his voice low and authoritative.

I glance back at Briony, who watches us with a dejected expression as Eldrion dismisses her with a wave of his hand. I want to reassure her, to tell her that I'll be all right, but the words stick in my throat as Eldrion strides away, expecting me to follow.

The stables are warm and musty, the scent of hay and horses filling my nostrils. Eldrion leads me to a large white horse, its coat gleaming in the dim light. He mounts his own steed, a magnificent black beast, and we set off into the night.

As we ride through the streets of the citadel, I can't help but notice the way people shrink back into their houses at the sight of Eldrion. Even with my empathic gates firmly shut, the fear he invokes is palpable, hanging heavy in the air like a suffocating fog.

We arrive at an inn on the outskirts of the citadel, a weathered wooden building with a faded sign hanging above the door. Inside, the air is thick with the scent of ale and sweat, and the low murmur of conversation fills the room. Eldrion orders two pints of ale and leads me to a table in the corner, where we sit in silence, seemingly waiting for something.

As the night wears on, the inn begins to empty, until we are the only patrons left. The innkeeper, a nervous-looking man with thinning hair, approaches our table cautiously. "Lord Eldrion," he says, his voice trembling slightly. "Can I fetch you some more ale?"

In a flash, Eldrion is on his feet, his hand slamming down on the table. He draws a knife from his belt and plunges it into the innkeeper's hand, pinning him to the wooden surface. The man cries out in pain, his eyes wide with terror.

"What do you know about *Vysoryn*?" Eldrion demands, his voice cold and menacing.

The innkeeper pleads with him, tears streaming down his

face. "I don't know what you're talking about, my lord. Please, I beg you, I know nothing of this demon."

Eldrion turns to me, his eyes boring into mine. "Drop your gates," he commands. "Tell me if he's telling the truth."

I hesitate for a moment, my heart racing in my chest. But I know I have no choice. I let my barriers fall away, and close my eyes. Taking off my gloves, I reach out and place one hand on the innkeeper's wrist. He flinches. His skin is cold and clammy. I inhale deeply. I do not need to touch him to know what he's feeling, but it helps. It grounds me.

Immediately, I'm overwhelmed by the man's fear and desperation. It swells inside me, tightens on the inside of my throat, claws beneath my skin. It is all-consuming. It makes me whimper. "Ask him again," I whisper.

Eldrion complies.

Again, the innkeeper says, "My lord, I swear, I don't know the word *Vysoryn*." His fear surges once again. Thick and black, like smoke coiling around his entire body. But then . . . beneath it all is the unmistakable flicker of deceit.

He's lying.

I open my eyes and meet the innkeeper's. Fear turns to terror as he searches my face. I tap his wrist lightly with my fingertips and sit back. Then I look at Eldrion. As I meet his gaze, I find myself saying, "He's telling the truth. He doesn't know what you're asking him."

For a long moment, Eldrion stares at me, his expression unreadable. I brace myself for his anger, for the accusation that I'm lying to him. But it doesn't come. Instead, he yanks the knife from the innkeeper's hand and sheathes it at his belt.

"We're done here," he says, his voice flat and emotionless as the innkeeper falls back in his seat, cradling his hand.

Outside, he jumps onto his horse and I do the same, swinging up instead of using my wings because it has always felt *right* to ride this way.

Stroking the horse's mane, I thank her for waiting for me.

Eldrion glances at me, his icy eyes shining in the darkness. Without speaking, he taps his horse's side and trots across the cobbles back towards the castle.

As we ride, I can't shake the feeling of unease that settles in the pit of my stomach. Eldrion trusted me, even when I lied to him. But why? Why would he trust me when I have every reason to deceive him?

"You took my gloves from my cabin." I turn and look at him through the darkness.

He does not look at me.

"They were in the bottom of my trunk at the foot of my bed. I know they are mine. The ones my mother gave me."

Eldrion makes a *hmm* sound deep in his throat.

"You knew who I was before you bought me at the arena." It is a statement, not a question, but he does not correct me. "How?"

This time, he does look at me. Arms loose at his sides, riding as if he can command his horse with only the grip of his thighs, he drags his gaze from my eyes to my lips.

Although I have shut off my empathy once more, I see it still . . . The way he trusts me. But there is something else, too.

Fear.

And suddenly, I know it was not just the innkeeper I felt; it was Eldrion, too.

He trusts me, but he is afraid of me, and I have no idea what that means.

ALTHOUGH BRIONY CLEARLY WANTS TO TALK TO ME ABOUT what happened, I ask her for some time alone, shut my door, strip off my clothes and my gloves, and lie down on the bed. The fire blazes in the grate. It is too hot in here – always too hot – and the heat is emphasised by the fact my body is trying to regulate itself after using the magic I so often keep guarded.

I stand up and throw open the window. Finally, there is a cool breeze outside, and I stand for a while, allowing it to calm my skin.

Vysoryn. Eldrion asked the innkeeper what he knew about *Vysoryn.*

I have never heard the word before, but whatever it means, it was important enough for him to take me out of the castle.

As my temperature descends back to something closer to normal, I take my robe from the back of the chair and slip it on. I examine the wound on my thigh. It healed perfectly just a day after Finn treated it, which – I have to admit – was disappointing because I had hoped he might come to check on its progress.

Perhaps Finn would know what *Vysoryn* means. He spoke to me in the old tongue when I met him at the centennial, and he is older than me – even if just by fifty or so years.

But what excuse can I find to see him again? Unless I get sick, it seems we are destined to simply stare at one another while he performs for the court.

I stride over to the fire, pick up the poker that sits beside the grate, and hold it in the flames. When I lift it out, I stare at its white-hot spike for a moment before snapping myself out of my madness and tossing it to the floor.

I should ask Briony. She would help if I asked her to. But somehow, it feels like my relationship with Finn – if it can be called a relationship – should be kept hidden.

Should be kept safe.

Just for me.

Thinking of him, trying to drag my mind away from Eldrion and what he wants from me and how I might use his trust to my advantage, I sit down in the armchair and close my eyes. I drift back to the waterfall. I see his blood-red mask, and feel his fingers tracing gently up my thighs.

Slowly, I run my hand down my neck, then open my robe. I moisten my fingers and then move them to my nipple and sigh as I pinch lightly.

My other hand is moving across my stomach when there is a tap-tap-tap on the door that jerks me back into the room.

"Briony, I asked to be alone." I stand, pulling my gloves roughly back onto my hands, and stride over to the door, annoyance stiffening in my limbs.

But when I open the door, it is not Briony on the other side – it is the jester.

Without speaking, he gestures for me to let him in, and I usher him silently inside. When the door closes, he stares into my eyes, grabs my waist, and kisses me. It is a deep, searching kiss, our mouths colliding as though they have been waiting for this moment for years instead of days.

"I'm so glad you're here," I breathe as I pull back and stroke the side of his mask.

"You weren't there tonight. I was worried. Briony said Eldrion took you somewhere."

I don't need to be an empath to see the worry in his dark brown eyes. I brush my thumb over his lips, then let him kiss my knuckles. "He did, but I'm all right."

"You don't have to tell me about it." Finn is stroking my arm. "But you can if you want to."

I shake my head, and reach up on tiptoes to kiss him again. "Not now." I take his hand and lead it to the opening of my robe. "For now, I need not to think, or talk. I just want to feel."

Finn's lips curl into a delicious smile. It sends lightning rods of pleasure down my spine to settle in my core and, not for the first time, I wonder how he's capable of doing that with only a look. Just a look.

"Do you think you can entertain me, jester?" I ask playfully, combing my fingers through his dishevelled hair.

Almost purring in response, Finn grabs my waist and tugs me into his chest. With his lips close to my ear, he whispers, "You're in luck, *si'thari* – entertainment is my specialty."

Chapter Eighteen

FINN

*I*n the darkness of her chambers, I drop to the ground and slide my hands up her legs. Her skin is like butter beneath my fingers.

"If Eldrion catches us, he'll kill you," she breathes. "Are you certain?"

I tighten my grip on her thigh. "I would die a thousand deaths if it meant I got to taste you. Just once." I grin up at her. "Besides, he won't catch us. No one knows I'm here."

"Briony knows."

"Briony can be trusted."

She falters, unable to think of any more reasons why I shouldn't touch her. She is wet and ready for me, lust dripping from her pussy because she has been thinking about this since the day we met in the forest.

Because she can feel how much I want her.

She nods at me, and I spin her around. She presses her hands flat to the wall.

As she waits for my tongue, her wings glow brighter, and the air pulsates with energy.

I lift her robe and palm her ass roughly, tugging a delightful hum from her lips.

Her sweetness is intoxicating. I breathe it in, pressing my face to the inside of her thigh. The last time we were together, I was only able to use my hands to please her. Now, I intend to use everything at my disposal.

I nuzzle into her scent.

I have never tasted a higher born fae before. Never dreamed a creature like her would even look at me, let alone fuck me.

My cock strains hard against my pants. I want her to touch me, but not before she has come on my lips.

"Finn . . ." My name drips deliciously from her tongue.

Finally, I give her what she wants; I breathe cool bursts of air over her clit, following them with my finger. Then I start to suck.

As I devour her, she melts into my mouth. I don't care if Eldrion finds us. I don't care if the whole castle hears how much I please her. In fact, I want them to hear.

I want them to know that I will do anything she asks of me. I want Eldrion to know I have claimed her before he has. Because that is undoubtedly his plan; for why else would he have tracked her down and brought her here if not because he is in love with her? Why else would he take her on secret trips outside the castle?

"Do you like that, *si'thari?*"

She reaches back and holds my head in place between her legs. "Good boy, don't stop."

Her praise sends a jolt of arousal to my balls. I groan loudly, and lap harder.

As her moans become more intense, her juices coat my lips and my chin. My fingers move in sync with my mouth, teasing her to the edge, feeling her body tense and coil as she thrusts her hips back to grind onto my face.

I can't help grinning as I grip her ass with one hand and slide the other down into my pants.

"Do I have your permission?" I ask.

She spins around to face me and looks down. Her eyes flit from mine to the bulge I desperately want to fist for her. "Yes," she says. "But don't come."

Breathless, lust coursing through my body and pooling at the base of my cock, I wrap my fingers around my shaft and moan into her quivering pussy as she hooks her leg over my shoulder.

Her wings pulse with an almost visible energy, warming the air between us. I reach up and run my finger along the lower rim of her right wing. She shudders and moans loudly, and my fingers fizz at the contact.

When I fuck her with my tongue, still stroking the under-side of her wing, she reaches down to circle her clit. She slams her fist into the wall, her body shakes, and she lets out a cry that echoes through the chamber, her wings fluttering wildly.

Her come floods my mouth, and I savour the taste, every last drop.

With a satisfied grin, I pull away and help steady her while her legs shake.

Staring at her, I slot my fingers into hers and raise her hand between us.

"Take these off," I breathe.

Her eyes widen and she shakes her head. "I can't."

"Tell me why you wear them." I squeeze her hand tightly.

She closes her eyes, the giddy haze of her orgasm fading quickly. "Because I hurt someone I loved."

Dipping my head, so she's forced to look at me, I hold her close. "Tell me what happened."

For a moment, she allows me to continue holding her, but then she pulls away and paces to the other side of the room, pulling her robe tightly around her waist. When she is positioned by the window, leaning with her back on the sill so she is facing me, she says, "I had the most incredible sex I'd ever had."

I raise my eyebrows, expecting her to look nostalgic. Instead, she simply looks devastated.

"It was the night Kayan asked me to marry him. We fucked under the stars. It wasn't the first time we'd done it, but it felt different. I was so lost in him that I lost control." She shudders visibly, and I cross the room to stand close to her.

"You lost control?" I tilt my head, trying to understand what she's saying.

"I felt for his emotions. To heighten my own. I wanted . . ." She laughs and shakes her head. "I wanted to feel what he was feeling as he fucked me. At first, it was incredible. Then I channelled some of it back to him, and it was incredible for him, too. We were in this bubble of euphoria, feeding each other's pleasure." Her eyes are wide, and her cheeks are flushed. "But then . . ."

Ignoring the pang of jealous in my gut, I prompt her to carry on. "Then?"

"Then it all went wrong. He started screaming. Pulled away from me. He was writhing on the ground, his wings flapping like a moth caught in a flame." She wipes a tear from her cheek and turns away from me to look out of the window. "I watched his entire body break in front of me. I took his magic. It drained right out of him, and left him a shell of what he was."

I swallow forcefully, and place my hands gently on her hips, leaning into her shoulder with my chin.

"I destroyed him. It took years for him to find himself again. He has his mind back now but . . ." She inhales sharply and hugs her own waist, gripping hold of my fingers as she does so. "His magic is gone. I took it."

When she turns around, she looks over my shoulder at my wings. "His wings are like yours now," she says. "No magic."

Mine flutter involuntarily, and I allow the bells on the tips to chime. "And you wear the gloves because you're afraid it will happen again?"

She hesitates, then says, "Not really. I know why it happened, even though I might not know *how*. If I brush against someone with my bare skin, it enhances their emotions. Amplifies them. Makes them brighter. It doesn't steal them." She examines the gloves as if she's seeing them for the first time. "I wear them because it makes others feel safer, and to remind me of what I did."

She is crying again. Thicker tears this time, and she sniffs as they roll down her cheeks.

I cup her face in my hands and stare into her eyes. "I have no magic for you to take." I grip her fingers with my own. "You cannot ruin me because I am already ruined."

Her mouth opens, and she shakes her head. She looks at her gloves. "I can't."

"Alana," I bark, causing her eyes to snap to mine and her lips to part in surprise. "Let me serve you. Let me show you all the ways I want to serve you. And let me start by showing you my heart."

She strokes the side of my mask, then kisses me in a way I have never been kissed before.

"I want to let you in," I whisper into her mouth. "Take what you need from me."

There is a pause and then, holding my gaze, Alana uses her teeth to pull off her gloves and drops them to the ground between us. "You really trust me not to hurt you?" she asks, her breath heavy in her chest.

My lips part and my hand returns to my cock. "You could never hurt me."

"Then, come here." Her eyes widen, feathers of heat dance on my skin.

She smiles, closes her eyes, and inhales deeply. When she opens them again, she dips her hand back between her legs and gathers some of her juices.

She raises her slickened fingers to her lips, opens her mouth, and sucks them inside. A moan of pleasure escapes her lips as she swirls her tongue over her fingertips, never taking her eyes from mine.

"Holy stars." I move urgently to kiss her, but she stops me.

"Would you like to come now?" she asks, trailing her wet finger down my bare chest, leaving a devastating trail of arousal in its wake.

Without answering, I grab her hips and carry her to the bed, spreading her legs wide, dragging the tip of my cock along her entrance and watching my pre-come merge with her wetness.

"You taste like heaven," I whisper, pulling down her dress to expose her breasts. "Don't you think?"

She grins at me. For a moment, I think I see a flicker of violet in her eyes. But it's gone so quickly, I wonder if it was just my imagination.

"You *feel* like heaven," she says, coiling her now-naked fingers around my thick erection.

I dip my head, suck her nipple into my mouth and swirl my tongue around it. While I am teasing her, she reaches between us, grabs my cock, and thrusts herself onto me. I groan loudly and grip the sheets above her head, then straighten myself so I can watch her face.

I need to watch her.

I need to see the way her eyes flicker as I fuck her.

With fierce determination, I thrust into her wet core. Her walls tighten around my cock with every stroke.

I grip her hips, the heat of her skin under my palms sending jolts of pleasure up my spine.

She moans softly, her wings pulsing in time with her breath as she reaches her arms back over her head and wriggles deeper into the mattress.

I pull out, slick from her pussy.

Her eyes snap towards mine, and her gaze narrows. "I didn't tell you to stop." She uses her legs to pull me back to her.

"Fuck, I love it when you talk to me like that," I murmur, positioning myself between her legs once more.

In the dim light, her eyes sparkle and her lips part with anticipation.

"I want you to come on my cock," I tell her. "I want to feel you come apart around me."

She nods, her eyes never leaving mine. "And I want to feel you come inside me."

I slide back in, and she arches her back as we find our rhythm again. The air crackles with energy. I thrust harder as her pussy constricts around me, teasing me with the promise of an orgasm.

I slam into her, the wet sounds of our bodies mingling with her cries, the strokes becoming more erratic, more desperate. I pull her closer, our bodies glistening with sweat.

She claws at my shoulders, then reaches back and tugs my left wing.

The sensation brings a jolt of pleasure and pain to my spine, and I cry out as my pierced tips chime for her.

"Let me feel you come," she breathes.

I thrust harder, my balls tightening, the tension building inside me like a tidal wave.

Her moans become louder, more urgent, and her wings flutter wildly.

Mine do too, and I grit my teeth, trying to hold back until the moment she permits me to release. "Now," she whispers, arching her back and grabbing the sheets beside her.

With a roar, I slam into her one last time, my body trembling with the force of my orgasm.

As I come, she gasps, tips her head back, then slams her naked hands onto my chest. Right above my heart. Her eyes widen, then roll back as her cheeks flush and her body unravels. She moans so loudly I swear the room starts to shake.

I explode inside her, filling her completely.

"I can feel you," she cries out. "It's like . . ." She loses her words and holds onto me as if she might fall even though she is pinned beneath me. She sighs as I continue to move within her. And with each wave of pleasure that washes over me, she whimpers as if she can feel it too.

We lie there panting and sweating, our bodies still joined together. She wriggles beneath me, unable to be still, smiling, cheeks flushed.

Finally, I pull out and collapse over her, my arms surrounding her. She strokes my hair as I catch my breath, her fingers moving through the damp strands. "I felt you," she says softly, her voice tinged with satisfaction.

"You've never done that before?" I ask, lacing my fingers with hers.

She shakes her head. She's staring at our intertwined hands. "Not since I lost control with Kayan."

"You lost control with me, too," I whisper, stroking a gentle line down between her breasts, over her stomach, her hips, her thighs. "But there's nothing you could take from me that I wouldn't willingly give you."

"I felt the way you wanted me." She shifts beneath my touch as if she still needs more of me, turning her face up to meet my eyes. "I felt your orgasm take over, felt it explode beneath your skin. Then it collided with mine and it was like fire inside me. So good it was almost painful."

She stifles a yawn and retracts her wings.

"Did you feel it? Was it different for you, too?"

I pull her close and kiss her forehead. "It was different," I smile. "But I don't think I felt what you felt."

She yawns again, her body softening as exhaustion takes over.

"Sleep . . ." I pull a blanket over her half-naked body. "I'll make sure no one sees me when I leave."

She murmurs a reply I can't quite hear, eyes heavy, already halfway below the veil of consciousness. I pause at the door and look back at her. Red hair splayed over the pillows, skin glowing with the remnants of her pleasure.

I fucked an empath.

An empath fucked me.

And now I know what it feels like, I know once will never be enough.

Chapter Nineteen

ALANA

NE WEEK LATER

"What do you talk about with him?" Finn asks, trailing his fingers over my collarbone in a way that makes my entire body shiver.

I lean into his embrace, resting my head on his shoulder. Not for the first time, I wish I had the courage to reach up and take his mask off his face.

It feels so strange to me that I know every inch of his body better than I know his face. That this is the one rule of Eldrion's that he will not break. That he is willing to sneak through the castle in the early hours of the morning to find me, he's willing to fuck me. He's willing to do all kinds of things that would get him into trouble, but he is not willing to remove his mask.

I have thought about searching his emotions at the same time as asking him why, so that I can tell whether he is offering me the truth in his answers. But I know that would be a betrayal, and I cannot do that to him.

Since we met, everything we've said to each other has been the truth.

I can't break that trust.

Slowly, I lace my fingers with his. I'm getting so used to not wearing my gloves with Finn, and when I'm with Eldrion, that putting them on now feels like a punishment.

For so many years, I wore them and didn't think about it. They became a part of me. And now, every time I slip them onto my fingers, I feel like I am participating in my own repression.

"He asks me about the magic Leafborne possess, about elemental magic, about my empathy." I glance up at Finn.

I still haven't told him what happened the night Eldrion took me to the inn. I haven't asked him if he understands what Eldrion asked the innkeeper about. And I haven't told him that Eldrion asked me to use my powers for him.

So, maybe I am breaking his trust already.

I shift uncomfortably, leaning closer to him as if his warmth can take away the pang of uneasiness that has settled in my belly.

Why haven't I told Finn about it?

We have talked about so many other things. Why not this? Perhaps it is because I don't want him to believe I am working with Eldrion or for him in any way. I also don't want to tell him something that could get him into trouble.

On top of that, there's no way of telling him what happened in the inn without telling him what I learned about Eldrion and his feelings towards me.

For, even now, when I enter Lord Eldrion's chambers, even when I have the gates of my empathy sealed tight, I see and feel what I felt then – he trusts me, but he is also wary of me.

And I still haven't figured out why.

"It seems strange that he would need you here to ask you such things," Finn ponders. "He has a castle full of academics and scholars, a library full of books. And he's the oldest fae in the kingdom. He knows all there is to know about magic."

I turn in Finn's arms and stroke his stubbled chin with my index finger. "What is *his* magic? Eldrion's?"

At that, Finn's entire aura stiffens. He sits up a little higher on the pillows, causing me to sit up too. "Eldrion has *all* magic," Finn says darkly.

Before I can ask what that means, he smiles and playfully tickles my shoulder.

"And, you know what? I believe he might be a little bit in love with you, Alana Leafborne. I believe *that is* why Lord Eldrion is taking you to his chambers every night . . . because he plans to corrupt you." Finn widens his eyes, chuckles deeply, and kisses my earlobe.

I pull away and roll my eyes, but his words have made my stomach constrict with unease.

"I do not believe Lord Eldrion is in love with me. But I do

believe there is more to these meetings than he's telling me," I say, changing the subject.

I sit up and reach for my robe.

It is not long until sunrise. But there is something I've been meaning to ask of Finn. And if I don't ask now, I will lose my nerve for the second night running.

"Will you take me to see the others?" I ask, sitting on the edge of the bed and trailing my fingers across his chest.

"The others?" he asks.

"I know they're still in the dungeons. They've been down there for nearly two weeks. No one will tell me what's happening to them."

Finn shakes his head, trying to reject the idea.

"I don't want them to think I've forgotten them. I want them to know I'm working on getting them out."

"Are you?" he asks solemnly.

"I'm building trust with Eldrion, trying to figure out what his game is. It's only been a short time, but if I stay steady and stay patient, I'm certain that I can find a way."

Finn cuts me off, sitting up abruptly and grabbing both of my hands. "Alana, you mustn't do anything that will put you in danger."

"So, I'm just to carry on doing this forever, am I?" I ask him, searching his face, even though it remains hidden beneath his mask. "Locked in here during the day, watching you perform in the evenings, talking with Eldrion at night, and then fucking you until sunrise."

"We make each other feel good," Finn says, inching closer to me and resting his hand on my thigh.

"We do. But that doesn't mean I can forget their plight, and I need them to know that."

Finn stands up, flexing his wings. His bells chime, and not for the first time, I realise that I've come to associate them with him, and that their subtle sound prompts heat between my legs.

"You really need to see them?" he asks, bracing his hands on his hips.

I nod firmly at him. "I really need to see them."

He looks at the window, then back at me. "All right," he says. "You're in luck. Henrik is on guard tonight, but we have to be quick. There's only a few hours till sunrise. We can't be caught wandering the castle when the guards switch over their duty."

I stand up, rush over to my wardrobe, and grab some clothes. "All right," I say, fetching my gloves too. "Let's go."

HENRIK, WHO I NOW KNOW IS BRIONY'S LOVER, LETS US into the dungeon while offering me a withering stare.

Immediately, the stench hits me. There is no light here, not a single window, and the low-ceilinged room is lit by only a few lamps.

The sound of bodies pressed together rustles in the corner.

I draw closer to the iron grate and take hold of the bars, wrapping my gloved fingers around them.

I peer into the gloom, and the silhouettes of my kin materialise into solid forms.

They're still chained.

I breathe slowly, my heart straining against my ribs, swelling with the horror of knowing this is how they have been for the last two weeks. While I've been comfortable in a bed with a fire, and a maid, and food, they have been here.

"Kayan," I whisper, "Are you there?" There is a clink of chains, and then Kayan comes into view.

His cheeks are sunken, and his eyes are grey.

Even his hair looks darker, no longer soft and wavy, but a dirty blond that hangs in greasy tendrils around his face.

He grips the chain as if it is helping to steady him and narrows his eyes at me.

"Alana," he asks, his voice hoarse, "is it you?"

I'm pressing my lips together, trying to find the words to tell him how sorry I am. But there are too many of them, and I can't put them in any sensible order. So, I just mutter, "Yes, it's me."

Kayan looks past me at Finn. "You brought her," he says. "You finally brought her."

Before I can ask what he means, Kayan returns his gaze to me and says, "You look well. He is treating you well."

I swallow, guilt dripping like acid down the back of my throat. "I'm not sure what he wants from me," I reply, "but he seems to trust me. He has been talking with me, asking me lots of questions."

From the shadows inside the cell, someone says, "And I suppose you have been giving him everything that he wants. Judging by the look of you, you're having quite a nice time while we all rot down here." I recognise the voice. It belongs to Maura, an elder who has hated me with a passion since the day I was born.

Guilt and shame hum on my skin.

For the first time since I was taken away, I genuinely wish I was still locked in here with them because at least then, perhaps they wouldn't hate me.

Finn appears at my elbow and puts a comforting hand on the small of my back, but I nudge him away when Kayan notices and say, "I'm going to do everything I can to get you out of here. I'm going to figure out a way. I can roam the castle. Eldrion knows I don't have the kind of magic that could fight back against him, but perhaps I can find a way for us all to get out. If I'm patient and careful and listen."

Kayan's lips twitch, and he tries to smile. "That sounds like a plan," he says. Then he adds, "And when we get out, maybe we can find Rosalie."

I rub my tongue on the roof of my mouth, trying to stop myself from crying.

I've thought about Rosalie every night since we got here. And every night, I've come to the same conclusion – that whatever is happening to her now is far worse than what's happening to any of us.

Some nights, my thoughts become so bad that Finn has to wake me up from a nightmare. But I've never told him what I'm dreaming about.

"Yes," I say, "we should do that."

"Oh, come on," Maura tuts. "Do you really think we're going to get out of here? Eldrion didn't want us. He wanted you. He's going to leave us here to rot, and don't pretend that you care. You've never been one of us."

"I've always been one of you. Even when you didn't want me to be."

Slowly, Maura steps forward. Her face is illuminated by the lamplight.

She was already old but now looks hundreds of years older. She rubs the chains around her wrist, then braces one arm across her stomach as if she's trying to quite literally hold her body together.

"No," she says, "your mother wanted you to be, but your father knew the truth."

"That's enough," Kayan interrupts her sharply. "Now's not the time."

"We should go," Finn whispers to me, taking hold of my elbow. "There's nothing you can do for them now. They don't want your help."

"I will help them," I tell him, and I turn back to them. "I will help you. I know you don't trust me. I know you don't like me. I know most of you have hated me since the minute I was born. Even before."

I look at Kayan, and he closes his eyes, unwilling to look at the shame on my face.

"But I swear, if I can get you out, I will."

"Come on." Finn tugs my elbow again.

Over by the door, Henrik grumbles, "He's right. Time to go."

I wait until I'm back in my chambers before I truly start to sob. Finn tries to comfort me, but I shake him off.

"I need to be alone," I tell him. "Please, just leave me alone."

He doesn't protest, just kisses me on the forehead. As he's leaving, he says, "If you really want to help them, then I'll do whatever you need me to, Alana. If that's what you want."

"It is what I want." I slowly remove my gloves and set them down on the table beside the bed.

"Then, tomorrow, we'll make a plan."

Chapter Twenty

ALANA

"*I* will not wait." I push back my chair and stand. Briony stares at me in alarm. "He wants me? He will see me now."

Ever since last night, the question, *What am I?* has been burning in my mind. Maura's words haunt me, circling round and round and round.

There is only one person who can answer this question.

One.

And I will not wait any longer to seek his answers.

She opens her mouth to protest, but I am already walking away and all she can do is scurry behind me.

When we reach his chambers, it is Henrik on duty. "You're early," he says, frowning.

"His request," I reply tightly.

Henrik looks at Briony for confirmation. She gives a small nod, her cheeks flushing. But instead of reading her blush as deceit, Henrik reads it as flirtation, and he smiles at her. "More time for us," he says, rolling his tongue over his upper teeth in a way that might be sexy if he was someone I found attractive.

Stepping aside, he gestures for me to enter. I push open the door and let it close quietly behind me. Through the thick wood, I can hear the murmur of conversation between Briony and Henrik which will, undoubtedly, soon become muted moans of pleasure as he fucks her up against the door.

The room is dark and silent. The fire flickers in the grate, but there is no sign of Eldrion. Usually, he greets me with a glass of whisky and lurches straight into his string of questions.

Now, he is nowhere to be seen.

I move deeper into the chamber. Clearly, this room is used as his living quarters and his study. Behind the fireplace, to the side, there is another door. A smaller one.

I approach slowly, my heart thundering in my chest. Suddenly, my bravado seems rather foolish.

I pause outside the door and press my ear to it.

Inside, a muffled sound escapes, a groan, low and guttural, like a beast in torment. It sends a shiver down my spine.

Then, he says my name. No, he doesn't *say* my name – he *moans* my name.

Heart pounding, I take a deep breath and turn the handle. The door opens silently. The room beyond is dimly lit, with shadows dancing on the wall and casting an eerie glow on Eldrion's figure.

He is standing by the window, facing away from me. One arm is braced on the wall, his wings spread wide and trembling. I creep into the room and slip into the shadows, moving until I can see past his wings.

CATCHING FULL VIEW OF HIS BODY, I SWALLOW A MURMUR of surprise.

HE IS COMPLETELY NAKED. AND WHILE HE PUNCHES THE wall with one fist, his other arm is moving in fast, jerky motions, his fingers curled tightly around a large, throbbing erection.

HE GROANS LOUDER, LETTING OUT A SHAKY BREATH. THEN he calls my name again, and treacherous wetness floods my core.

How can I want him so badly when I fear him so much? When I fear his power, his control over me, and the darkness that lurks in his soul.

"He is evil," Briony said. "He has done unspeakable things."

And yet this evil, dark, all-powerful creature is using my name to bring him to climax.

My fingers find the hem of my dress and slide it up my thighs, my gaze fixed on the twisted shapes that his wings cast on the wall.

Eldrion's muscles ripple as his hips thrust forward, the

sound of his laboured breathing mingling with the soft whisper of the wind outside the window.

As the room swirls with shadow and light, I lose myself in the rhythm of my name on his lips, aching to touch the damp heat between my legs.

A low growl escapes his lips, and he turns his head.

FOR A MOMENT, I CANNOT BREATHE BECAUSE I AM CERTAIN he has seen me, but then he closes his eyes, releases another loud moan, and tightens his grip on his cock.

MOVING MY UNDERWEAR TO ONE SIDE, I SLIP MY FINGERS past the lace and begin to circle my clit. My nipples are hard, straining against the silk fabric of the corset I wear beneath my dress. My breath quickens, but I do not close my eyes. I keep them on him.

I WATCH HIS SHOULDERS RIPPLE, AND HIS STOMACH TENSE. I see the veins in his arms, and the way his breath hitches as pleasure builds inside him.

"FUCK, ALANA . . ." HE TURNS AROUND, AWAY FROM THE window, and the hand that was braced against the wall throws a bundle of light into the centre of the room.

MY FINGERS SLOW. I CANNOT BREATHE.

. . .

FOR THERE, SUSPENDED IN THE MIDDLE OF THE ROOM, IS A shimmering vision of a body I recognise.

MY BODY.

I AM NAKED, TIED TO A WALL WITH CHAINS AROUND MY wrists. And Eldrion is in front of me. As he stalks towards me, his silver hair moves softly over his shoulders. He roughly takes my chin in his hand, then kisses me.

AND IT IS AT THAT MOMENT I REALISE I AM NOT A PRISONER in his vision but a lover.

HE KISSES ME DEEPLY, THEN DRAGS HIS LIPS DOWN MY throat to my naked breasts. He sucks one nipple playfully into his mouth, kneading it with his expert tongue.

AS I WATCH, MY FINGERS RETURN TO MY CLIT AND ELDRION – the real one, the one who is standing just feet away from me watching the same thing I am – starts jerking his cock once more.

HE STANDS, STOCK-STILL, WATCHING THE VISION PLAY OUT.

IS HE DOING THIS? IS THIS WHAT HE WAS PICTURING WHEN he was standing by the window?

· · ·

THE VERSION OF ME THAT IS CHAINED UP WRAPS HER LEGS around Eldrion and cries out as he enters her. I stifle a moan, biting the back of my hand so hard I draw blood.

THEN THE VISION DISAPPEARS. ELDRION DROPS TO HIS knees and comes hard onto the floor, hot come drenching the stone beneath him.

He stays there a moment, breathing hard, then sits back on his knees and scrapes his hand through his hair.

It is when he smiles that my orgasm takes over.

BECAUSE IT IS THE FIRST TIME I HAVE SEEN HIM LOOK anything other than deadly.

He smiles, and shakes his head. "Fuck, that woman. She will end me," he mutters.

AND WITH THAT, MY BODY UNCOILS.

WHEN ELDRION FINALLY EMERGES FROM HIS BEDROOM, I AM sitting in his armchair, legs crossed.

I greet him with a rather cocky stare, but he seems oblivious to its meaning.

If I hadn't known what was happening a moment ago, there would be no visible signs of it anywhere on his face or his body.

Fully clothed now, he walks over to the table where he keeps his whisky and pours himself a glass.

"I want you to tell me who I am," I waste no time and speak firmly, feeling a newfound sense of assurance that he will not hurt me because a man who calls my name like that could surely not hurt me.

Eldrion takes a slow sip from his whisky. "You're an empath," he says.

"An important one," I counter.

My words are more of a statement than a question, but Eldrion tilts his head from side to side and says, "Perhaps."

"You tracked me down in my village long before you brought me here."

Eldrion chews his lower lip. "I did."

"Why?"

"I cannot tell you that, not yet."

Again, I ask, "Why?"

Eldrion's eyes flash and he drums his fingers on his glass. "Are you a child?" he says, his voice like gravel in the back of his throat. "Always asking why, why, why."

"You bought me at auction, gave me chambers in your castle, and have spent every night for nearly two weeks questioning me on things you already know about. You took me outside the castle and made me use my powers against an innocent man. And you're afraid of me."

I stand up to meet his stare.

He glowers down at me, his eyes glittering like diamonds, sharp and deadly and beautiful.

"You have searched my feelings?" he asks darkly.

"No," I say, "I have not. But some of them crept in when we were with the innkeeper. I didn't realise it at first; I thought it was all him. But the tendrils of darkness I felt, they were you, weren't they?" I tilt my chin up towards him, fire rising in my belly. "How can you, the most powerful fae in the kingdom, be afraid of me? A fae with so little magic that you allow me to roam your castle unrestrained while my friends rot in your dungeon."

"They're not your friends," he says. "They will never be your friends. They did not understand you or appreciate you. They do not trust you. They do not know what you are. You offered to free them, and still they do not trust you."

I stifle a sharp intake of breath. How does he know? Finn? Henrik? They would not betray me, for they have done things that would get them in far deeper trouble.

But then how?

In one quick stride, Eldrion closes the gap between us.

He flexes his wings so wide that a shadow falls over me, and I think he's going to wrap them around me. "It is you who should be afraid of me," he growls.

My heart thunders in my chest. Am I afraid of him? Perhaps I was, but now, in this moment, I'm simply curious.

A sudden, tremulous knock on the door causes Eldrion to look up and stride away from me.

He flings it open in a way that makes me think he's going to strangle whoever is on the other side, but when he looks down and finds Briony blinking up at him, his expression softens just a tiny bit.

"What is it?" he barks.

"Trouble," she whispers, her voice shaking. "The dungeons, my lord. Trouble."

Eldrion strides back to me, grabs my hand, and drags me towards the door.

Briony mouths, "I'm sorry," in my direction, but I'm whisked past her before I can ask what she is sorry for.

We have not even reached the staircase that leads to the cells when I hear the screaming.

Chapter Twenty-One

KAYAN

*I*t has to be tonight. We cannot wait any longer. "I heard them talking about moving us," I whisper quickly. It is late. Everyone is gathered around, but we only have until Briony stops moaning Henrik's name until we have to stop and resume our positions.

It happens like this every night. As soon as she has deposited Alana with Eldrion, Briony comes here, fucks Henrik, then runs back up in time to take Alana back to her chambers.

"We should do it as soon as he's back." I glance at Raine. "You're sure about this?"

She nods, resting her hands on her stomach. "I am not giving birth in this cell," she says. "So if I have to fake some contractions to get us out of here. Then, yeah, I'm sure."

I smile at her, but I can feel Maura's eyes boring into me like daggers. "It's too risky," she says.

"No, it's not. Henrik is our sole guard. No one else will be in danger. He'll open the cell, and when he examines Raine, I'll attack."

A flurry of voices rise up, and I have to hush them quickly. Most are in agreement. Only a few believe we should wait and be cautious.

"Right now, we know Henrik's routine. We know this place and its movements. If we're moved, we could be separated or worse. And next time we might not have just one hapless guard to contend with. We could have more than one." I pause and turn to Maura. "*But* as the only elder present, Maura, you have final say. I will not do anything without your blessing."

Maura sucks in her cheeks. Fury blooms across her cheekbones. "You have made up your mind," she says. "I won't pretend I think trying to stop you will do any good."

"Then you agree?" I ask, my hand twitching in my pocket.

Maura sighs. "I agree." She answers me with closed eyes, and when I nod at the others to prepare themselves, she leans in close and takes my hand. "I know why you're doing this, though, Kayan. And I know it has nothing to do with us changing location."

I hesitate, fiddling with the discarded fishbone I spent the last week fashioning into a sharper point.

She meets my eyes, her lips a thin foreboding line. "You're doing this for *her*. Because *she* wants to rescue us and you don't want her to be hurt."

I open my mouth to object. At the same time, my thumb pricks the fishbone and I wince. "Both things can be true."

I take out the bone and deftly unfasten the magic binders from my wrists.

Maura makes a *hmm* sound in the back of her throat, but clearly chooses not to say anymore because she turns away from me and laces her fingers together as if she's praying. Perhaps she is, because I'm sure I see her lips twitching. Uttering words of the old tongue to wish us luck and good fortune.

"They're done," Pen hisses. He is closest to the door side of the cage and also has a keen sense of hearing. It was him who heard Henrik and the other guard, Bran, talking about moving us.

A few moments later, the door clatters back and Henrik strides back in, adjusting his trousers. There is no sign of Briony, but she will be on her way back to Alana. To wait outside while she and Eldrion . . . do whatever it is they do in their nightly sessions.

Henrik assesses us carefully, checks we're all roughly where he left us, then grunts that it'll be lights out soon and we should be getting some sleep. Right on cue, as he walks away, Raine begins her performance.

First, a wince. Then a shuffling of discomfort. A groan and then, the true stroke of genius, behind her someone throws a splash of water from our ration bottle. By the time Henrik turns around, Raine is clutching her stomach, panting, and begging for help.

"Please," she says, eyes wide. "It's too early. The baby isn't due yet."

Henrik's mouth drops open. Still in the flush of his tryst

with Briony, he stutters, hesitates, and when Raine starts to double over in pretend waves of pain, runs to the bars.

"Please, help me," Raine pleads.

"I can't." Henrik brushes his hand through his hair. His face is pale and sweaty. "I'm so sorry, I can't."

"At least unfasten her chains, so I can deliver the baby." Maura speaks up, pulling herself to her feet. "I am the only one here with enough experience and I'm not close enough."

"Tell them what to do." Henrik waves his hand at those closest to Raine.

"She can't give birth in chains." Maura tilts her chin up defiantly. "Young man, do you have a mother? A sister? A lover?"

Henrik glances at the door, so quickly it's almost unnoticeable. But clearly he's thinking of Briony. "I . . ."

Maura stands firm, while I try to make myself as invisible as possible. Right now, all Henrik should be thinking about is the pregnant mother who needs help and the kind old fae woman who has offered it.

Eventually, he nods, fumbles for his keys, and pulls open the door. He strides over to Raine and unfastens her chains. She mutters a strained thank-you and sinks to her knees.

"Hang on, Raine, I'm coming." Maura holds out her hands.

Henrik stands between Maura and me, back to me, and puts the key into the cuff around her neck. It clicks open. But before he can turn around, I jump for him. Wrapping my entire body around his, I bring my weapon to his throat and press it against his skin until a bead of blood bubbles up from its stubbled surface.

Maura grabs the keys from him and throws them to Raine, who instantly starts unlocking everyone else.

"You won't get away with this," Henrik says. Then he adds, "You won't even make it over the bridge. The sentinels will see you and they'll shoot arrows at you until you're —"

"Which is why you're coming with us," I spit. "Leverage."

At that, Henrik laughs. He laughs so hard, I feel his ribs move beneath me. "You think they'd let you free to save *my* life?" He squirms beneath me but I keep hold of him, surprised by how much desperation has fuelled my strength. "They couldn't care less about me, you fools."

"Which is why we need the cuffs off, too." I nod at Pen. Now unchained, he marches out of the cells and begins to raid Henrik's desk. "There's nothing here," he says. "I thought they were . . . We saw them. The keys. They're always in here."

I tighten my grip on Henrik. "Where are they?"

"There is no point," he says, with almost a hint of a sigh.

"Where *are* they?"

There's a pause, and then he says, "All right. I'll show you."

Slowly, still holding my weapon at his throat, I march him out of the cell. But we haven't even crossed the threshold before he turns on me. Wrenching round in my grasp, cutting his own throat, but not deep enough to wound him badly, he knocks the weapon from my hand and punches me hard in the stomach. I try to fight him off, but he is bigger and stronger.

He batters me to the ground. I yell at the others to stay back and concentrate on finding the keys to the binders. He has his hands around my throat when the door clatters back on its hinges and Briony's sweet voice calls, "Henrik!"

The split second in which he looks for her is enough to give me an advantage. I use his body weight against him, flip him over, and pin him to the ground. "Let us go. Help us," I say, staring into his eyes.

I expect him to go limp beneath me. To relent. But he doesn't. So, when Maura puts the weapon back into my hand, I don't hesitate.

I thrust it into his gut and twist.

Chapter Twenty-Two

ALANA

*E*ldrion lingers at the top of the spiral staircase.

Thunderous footsteps move towards us, and he steps aside as two bulky guards I don't recognise emerge holding a figure between them.

When I realise who it is, my hands fly to my mouth.

In the back of my mind, it occurs to me that I'm not wearing my gloves, and yet I can't care about that now because the person they are holding is Kayan.

Screams, cries, and commotion filter up from the dungeons.

Eldrion slams the door shut and demands, "Tell me what is happening."

The guard on the left, a female with dark brown hair and deep blue eyes, says, "He attacked one of us. We were hosing them down because they stink," she spits, "and he attacked us. He had fashioned a weapon, managed to unhook his chains —"

"Which guard?" Eldrion interrupts.

The woman falters. Her brusque demeanour wavers a little, then she says, "Henrik. He's dead." Behind me, Briony whimpers and backs up against the wall.

Eldrion breathes heavily. He rolls his tongue over his upper teeth. His wings twitch.

Kayan is bleeding from his head, and his eye is swollen. He hangs limply between the guards, barely moving, barely breathing.

My heart thunders. My entire body feels like it might implode, but I force it to move.

Stepping between Kayan and Eldrion, I stop short of grasping his hands but stare up at him and whisper, "My lord, please don't hurt him."

My words hang in the air between us. There is utter stillness.

Eldrion stands stock-still, breathing slowly, his shoulders rising and falling, his wings twitching.

He tears his gaze away from me and, looking only at Kayan, says, "Take him to the parapet and ring the bell."

The guards nod quickly and turn, dragging Kayan lifelessly between them to ascend another set of stairs that lead up instead of down.

This time, I do grab Eldrion's arm. "What's happening? What are you going to do to him?"

He cranes his head slowly to look down at me, looks at my gloveless hand, then rips his arm away from me so hard I am sent flying. Only my wings stop me from hitting the ground.

Still, he doesn't answer me, just turns and looks at Briony.

She is sobbing, hugging her waist. It seems Henrik was more than just a lover. He was her love.

"Take her outside so she can see," Eldrion says, his words slow and dark. They nestle like shards of ice between my ribs.

Shaking, Briony nods. She takes hold of my hand, and I want to protest, but something about the way she holds on stops me.

Outside, it is cold and dark.

Lanterns flicker around the parapet of the castle.

We stand alone, and I put my arm around Briony's waist as the wind whips across our faces.

Then, a bell tolls five times.

As the final toll echoes into the night, signs of movement begin within the citadel.

Shadowkind servants emerge from the castle, and Sunborne filter their way up from the streets and from the Grand Hall to stand nearby.

It is as if everyone knows what is about to happen except for me, and yet I don't ask.

We stand silently, and I search the crowd for Finn but cannot find him.

When Briony squeezes my hand, I follow her gaze up towards the parapet.

The unmistakable silhouette of Lord Eldrion has appeared. He spreads his wings out wide, and his voice booms, "Death to all traitors!"

Suddenly, loudly, deeply, everyone around me echoes his chant, "Death to all traitors!"

Even Briony mutters it beneath her breath.

Nausea swells in my gut.

I want to look away because something deep inside me tells me what's about to happen, but I can't because Kayan is there, too.

Eldrion turns to face him. He might be speaking, but from here, I can't tell. I can't see his lips moving, and I can't hear him.

Everything is quiet, then there is another rustle of movement; the Leafborne from the dungeon are being herded out here, too.

They are pushed and shoved to the very front of the crowd, surrounded by at least ten guards holding them in place. Their heads are jerked back, so they are forced to look up. Every single one of them is sobbing.

Then I feel him. Finn. Behind me.

I'd know his energy anywhere, and though I can't look at him or touch him, I lean into his warmth as if he alone can keep me from falling to my knees.

Without saying another word to the crowd below, Eldrion beats his wings, takes hold of Kayan with just one hand, and lifts him into the air.

He flies higher, holding Kayan so they are suspended above us.

Then, with his other hand, he rips out Kayan's wings.

Kayan's scream pierces the air and my heart.

I cannot breathe. I cannot see. Tears and darkness and pain swell behind my eyes as Kayan's wings catch light and become nothing more than ashes on the breeze.

He writhes in Eldrion's grip.

Still, Eldrion holds on to him with only one hand. Then, with the other, the one that ripped off his wings, he reaches for a knife and slits Kayan's throat.

He holds him still while his blood drips down his body.

It falls slowly through the air, and by the time it reaches the ground, it barely makes an impact.

Eldrion keeps him there until the bleeding stops, until our necks ache from looking up, until our hearts burn and our bodies feel like crumbling.

Then, he lets him fall.

Chapter Twenty-Three

ALANA

I am shaking. I cannot speak, and I cannot see straight. My entire body is racked with a pain so visceral I can't breathe.

I hear it again and again. The scream when Kayan's wings were ripped from his body, and then the thud when he landed on the ground.

Bent.

Broken.

Gone.

Finn and Briony dragged me back to my chamber kicking and screaming. "We can't leave him there! We can't leave him!" Now, Briony hands me a glass of whisky and takes one for herself.

Smoothing my hair from my face, Finn tries to make me look at him but I screw my eyes shut and turn away. "Why did he do it? I told him I'd help. I told him I'd set them free. Why would he risk it?"

I hear it again.

Rip.

Scream.

Thud.

"What will he do to the others?" I look from Finn to Briony.

She has stopped crying, and her voice comes out as nothing more than a reedy whisper. "I don't know, my lady."

"I have to see them." I stand and stride to the door. "Take me to them, now."

Finn and Briony exchange a look of shock and disbelief. "Alana, that is not a good idea. Not now. Not tonight."

"If you do not take me, I will take myself." I throw open the door and run, and I don't care if they are following me or not.

By some miracle, I make it to the stairs without meeting a single other soul. The castle is quiet. It is as if everyone is mourning, except they are not. No one cared for Kayan. The Sunborne saw his death as simply an added bonus to the night's entertainment, and the Shadowkind in Eldrion's employ just sighed and hung their heads. As if they were thinking, *foolish boy, we knew this would happen.*

The cells are unguarded.

I do not care to wonder why.

I run to the iron bars and shake them. There is silence within. No one speaks.

"What happened? What did you do? I told you I'd help." I am shouting but still no one answers me. "Tell me what happened, damn you!"

Maura is the one who steps forward. She is not in chains. None of them are. Clearly, Eldrion believes they have learned their lesson. "Kayan . . ." She chokes on the sob that racks her chest. "He had a plan."

In the darkness, all I can hear is the sound of the others crying. Holding one another. Broken.

None of us can unsee what we saw tonight.

I press my head against the bars. I want to tell them I'll still find a way to free them. But the words catch in my throat and refuse to be spoken.

"Alana . . ." Finn puts his hand on mine, and I flinch. A surge of guilt washes over me as I think of what I did while I was watching Eldrion.

"It's all my fault," I whisper. "All of this. It's my fault."

Finn tweaks a finger beneath my chin. "Do you want to help them?" he asks quietly.

I frown at him. "Of course, I do."

He glances back at Briony. She is guarding the door.

"Then there is something you can try. I've seen empaths do it before."

I let go of the bars and turn away from Maura and the others. "What can an empath do to get them out of here?"

"It won't set them free of the dungeon, but you can set them free of their pain." Finn presses his hand to my chest, above my heart, and smiles a slow smile. "You can take their pain from them. Absorb it from them."

"All of them?" A violent shiver snakes down my spine.

"It's a lot, but I believe you can do it. If you weren't power-ful, Eldrion wouldn't have brought you here."

I close my eyes, breathe slowly and steadily, then push back my shoulders and take his hand. "How? Show me how . . ."

"I CAN'T," FINN SAYS, HIS LIPS TWITCHING A LITTLE AS HE almost smiles. "When I saw another empath do it, they closed their eyes, waved their hands and –"

I laugh darkly. "And what? Sparkly lights flew out of their fingertips?"

He shrugs. "Something like that. Their wings glowed. The air started to glow. It kind of spread over the person –"

"Person? Just one person? You saw an empath do this for one person, and now you expect me to do it for twenty?"

Finn's eyes soften. He looks a little bit like a child, as if I just reprimanded him, and he feels embarrassed. "I'm sorry."

I take his hand and squeeze it tightly because he is the only person here who sees me for who I really am, and who wants me anyway. "I just don't know if I can."

"Alana," he leans in close, whispering into my ear, "Eldrion would not have brought you here if he didn't believe you were special."

It's the second time he has said this to me, and this time, I know he's right.

"Last time I took something away from someone, it was —" I can't finish my sentence. The words simply will not leave my mouth.

I don't think I will ever be able to say Kayan's name again or think of him without hearing those sounds and seeing his poor, broken body.

The thought that he is no longer in this world makes me want to vomit onto the floor at my feet. The thought of escaping here, and finding Rosalie, and having to tell her that he has gone makes me want to vomit harder.

"Is it right to stop them from grieving?" I ask.

"You're not stopping them from grieving," Finn says. "You're taking the worst of it, the most painful parts, that's all."

I try to force myself to breathe, but it's like the air is getting trapped in my lungs and doesn't know how to escape.

I start to pace up and down.

Something deep inside is telling me that he's right, that I can do this. I just don't know how.

My entire life, I've been told to suppress my magic. No one has ever taught me how to embrace it or use it. All it has brought is darkness.

I breathe out slowly, brush my hair over my shoulders, and rub my face with my palms. Then I flex my fingers at my sides, brace myself, and lower the gates in my mind.

Immediately, a flood of emotion hits me. It is so strong, I quite literally fall to my knees.

But when Finn moves to help me, I gesture for him to stay away.

Maura has moved to the bars and is watching me carefully. Some of the others do too, but none of them speak. She tilts her head, looking at me curiously, as if she's never really seen me before.

I meet her eyes. "I'm going to help you," I say.

"I don't want your magic anywhere near me," she spits, the vitriol rolling off her tongue along with her saliva. But beneath it, like grains of sand in the deepest depths of the ocean, is a heartbreaking sadness that makes me want to embrace her, even though she hates me.

Fear and sadness swell in the air around me. They press down on my skin and burrow their way into my soul. They are so overwhelming, I can barely breathe.

I reach out my hands.

I don't know why, but it feels like the right thing to do.

I splay my fingers, and there it is – a small ball of purple light.

Maura steps back from the bars; the others do too. "Stop that," she says. "Whatever you're doing, stop."

But I ignore her. My wings are starting to flutter. I feel them glow, too, and I rise to my feet. The purple light in my hands dissipates, becomes thinner. It dissolves into the air and spreads like a blanket over the entire cell.

They watch it, transfixed. Even Maura now does not move. She just holds out her arms as the purple light lands like feathers on her skin.

I glance at Finn. He's watching me in awe.

I move closer to the bars, holding my arms out so my palms are facing the Leafborne in the cell, and I close my eyes. I imagine dragging the light back inside me, pulling their pain and their fear and their sadness and all the darkness that consumes them into me instead.

It hits me like a tsunami and sends me flying. My back slams into the wall, grazing my wings, and I drop to the floor.

My entire body starts to shake.

I cough, clutching at my chest.

My insides feel like they're burning.

In my mind, the pain feels as though it's about to split my skull in half. Then there is another burst of light. It comes from deep inside me, emanating from every pore, filling the room. And then it is gone.

Silence descends.

I look over at the cell. It is silent there too. No one is crying.

Maura meets my eyes and wraps her willowy fingers around the bars as she stares out at me.

"Thank you," she says.

Chapter Twenty-Four

ALANA

Finn kneels in front of me and places his hands on my knees. Tears stain my cheeks and congeal in my throat, and I hurt so much I can hardly move. He squeezes lightly until I look at him.

"You took away their pain." He smiles from beneath his mask. "You did good, Alana. You did a good thing."

"But it hurts so much." I press my fingers to my temples. I feel like my skull might explode.

"So, now let me help you." He stands and cradles my face in his hands, brushing my tears with his thumbs.

Finn's touch is gentle, like the flutter of a moth's wings against my skin. I close my eyes and let myself lean into his warmth, seeking solace in the darkness behind my eyelids. When I open them again, his eyes bore into mine with such intensity that it feels like he's peering into the very depths of my soul.

"I can make it stop hurting, Alana," he whispers. "The way you did for them."

I nod wordlessly. I would do anything not to feel like this anymore.

Finn moves away from me, and heads for the curtains. I watch, confused, as he unfastens the large rope ties that hold them back and, instead, winds them around his hands.

The dim light casts elongated shadows across the room, and suddenly, everything about the way he is moving seems different. Darker. More forbidden.

"I'm going to teach you how to bind my wings," Finn says, his voice low and hypnotic. "And then you can do whatever you like with me. I'll be yours. You'll have all the power. You can use me until you don't hurt anymore."

His words seep into my skin and send shivers of anticipation through my veins.

I watch as he unfurls the rope, its fibres rough against my skin as he places it in my hands. My fingers tremble slightly as I take hold of it, the weight of his words settling heavily in my chest.

He kneels in front of me and stretches out his wings. "Press them against my body."

I do as he says, and although he's the one teaching me, I am the one with the power.

I feel it, and I see it in his eyes.

"Curl them tightly around my arms." He winces as I follow his instructions, enjoying the sensation of manipulating his body with my hands. "Now, the rope."

With each movement, each twist and knot he shows me, each jerk of tension that makes him groan, I feel more powerful. And less broken.

As the last knot is secured, Finn looks up at me. His wings are wrapped tightly around his body, pressing his arms at his sides. He can move his legs, but not his torso.

Reaching down, I take the piece of rope that hangs between his arms and secure his wrists, too. His eyes widen as I do so, and he dips his head in submission.

The air in the room grows thick with tension.

I know what I'm going to do next.

Sliding my hands down the side of his face to his neck, I can feel his pulse thrumming beneath my fingertips, a steady rhythm that matches the pounding of my own heart. I tighten my grip on his throat, and watch as he closes his eyes and gives into me.

When I stop, he opens them again and I see a flicker of something primal that matches the hunger in my core.

Roughly, I push him back against the cold stone floor. He untucks his legs from beneath him and lies there, bound for me, offered up for my pleasure.

I straddle his waist and slide my hands up his chest, over the knots, and the fragile veins of his wings. I stroke the piercings on his tips, and sigh as they chime gently for me. Then I reach for his mask.

Finn inhales sharply, and flinches.

"You are mine," I whisper. "And I want to see your face."

He says nothing in response, just closes his eyes and remains completely still while I unfasten it and lift it free.

In the flickering orange light of the chamber, his face is everything I thought it would be. His jaw is strong and firm, and his cheekbones are, too. I stroke his features slowly and carefully, as if I'm trying to learn every inch of him by heart.

When I reach the mottled scar on his cheek, and stroke it with my thumb, he releases a low humming sound and turns his face away from me.

I bring it back, then lower my lips to his skin and try to kiss away whatever memory haunts him.

At first, Finn resists, but then his body arches beneath mine and I explore every inch of him with a hunger that borders on obsession.

I remove his pants, and toss them aside.

The taste of salt and sweat graces my tongue as I move my way up his bare legs towards his cock.

But I don't touch him there. Not yet.

I play with him, using my lips and my hands to claim him.

Finally, thrusting my mouth onto his shaft, I fill myself until my eyes water and he groans loudly. I sit back, smiling.

I am not doing this to give him pleasure; this is for me, and he is letting me take what I need.

Again, I take him in my mouth. And again, and again.

I bring him to the edge of an orgasm, and then let it fade away. And when he can't take any more, I lower myself onto him, grip him with my thighs, and let him thrust up into me until he explodes.

With his come dripping from my pussy, I move to his lips. "Can you taste yourself?" I whisper.

He moans into my clit.

"Do you taste good?"

He laps and circles and groans.

I scrape my fingers through my hair and arch my back. My body coils tightly, pressure building. I lean back and tug the rope that holds his wings in place, and the sound he makes finally sends me over the edge.

Fire explodes beneath my skin. My wings flutter violently.

As it subsides, and I return to my body, I realise he was right; some of the hurt has gone. And it has been replaced by strength.

Chapter Twenty-Five

ELDRION

*W*hen everyone is back inside, I leave the parapet and descend to the ground.

My wings beat hard, then stop. I land with a thud that kicks dirt up into the air. Behind me, the castle is silent and swollen with fear.

This is not the first time I have performed a midnight execution, and I doubt it will be the last. For it seems they never learn. They must always push back, test my strength. And I am always forced to prove to them who is in control.

The boy lies, body broken, at a strange angle. Like a shattered marionette, he is completely lifeless now. Not that he had much of a life before.

Perhaps that is why he did it; because he felt he had nothing to lose. Or because he felt he wouldn't be watched too carefully.

The reason doesn't matter. What matters is he tried to betray me. He killed one of *my* guards. A guard I took from a Shadowkind orphanage and raised to be exactly what I needed.

No one takes what is mine and gets away with it.

I stoop down, and push Kayan's blond hair from his face. It is a weak face with no discernably interesting features. How she could ever fall for this creature, I have no idea.

I sigh and scoop the boy into my arms. His limbs flop loosely as I fly up into the air and over the buildings that surround the castle. It is high tide. At this time of night, the citadel is locked in by water. Cut off from the rest of Luminael. The way I like it.

When I reach the part where the water is deepest, and where he will be carried out into the ocean when the tide goes out, I hover for a moment.

I close my eyes and mutter the words we always mutter when someone dies. Then I send him plummeting into the icy depths of the Luminael sea. His body lands with a splash and is instantly submerged. She will be sad that there is no grave. But I cannot allow myself to care what Alana Leafborne feels.

When I return to the castle, I go straight to my chambers and into the room I keep hidden even from my most trusted aides. Accessed via the bookcase at the back of the living quarters, it is small and dark.

I exhale slowly, and my magic surges to life.

In here, I can let it be everything. I can let it surge without fear of revealing too much of myself.

The walls crackle with electric energy. Miniature lightning rods fork across the ceiling. I reach out and brace my hands on the walls; the room is small enough that I can touch each side of it without needing to stretch.

I release a deep, primal roar and feel the stone shake beneath my fingers.

When I open my eyes, I mutter the incantation that will show her to me.

And there she is . . . a shimmering vision in the centre of the room. Bright against the pure, inky blackness of my secret space. Exactly as I anticipated, she is not in her chamber. Instead, she is making her way quickly through the castle.

And, of course, she is with him.

The jester.

They head for the dungeons. As I requested, there are no guards on duty. Because if there was ever a time for Alana to show me what she is capable of . . . it is tonight.

When Finn suggests that she can take their pain away, I study her eyes carefully. She doesn't believe it, and why would she? Her magic has been oppressed for so long, she's forgotten what it feels like. But empathy is powered by emotion.

Right now, she has all the power she needs. It is thickening in her veins, pumping fast through the deepest parts of herself. She just needs to access it.

Finn gives her a pathetically inadequate explanation of what he saw when another empath attempted to take away a person's emotions. He is a poor teacher, but then he is Shadowkind and has lived a cloistered life here in the castle. So, his failings are to be expected.

As I watch the scene unfolding, my heart races. Alana hesitates, doubt etched upon her face.

I lean forward as she begins to pace, wrestling with the decision to embrace a side of herself she was always told to ignore. Then something shifts. I see it. A flicker of violet in her eyes.

And in that moment, I know exactly what is about to happen.

As Alana lowers the gates in her mind, I clench and unclench my fists. The flood of emotion that engulfs her is palpable. She falls to her knees, overwhelmed by the sheer force of the Leafbornes' pain and sorrow.

This is it. All she needs to do is take that pain, and use it.

My breath catches in my throat as Alana extends her hands.

She knows what to do, even though she has never been taught.

A small ball of purple light appears. The light grows, spreading like a blanket over the entire cell. The prisoners, even Maura, stand transfixed by Alana's ethereal glow.

It settles on them like snow, melting into their skin, and they watch it in awe while I watch Alana. She doesn't know it, but she is glowing too.

Her wings shimmer, her face brightens, and there's that flash of violet in her eyes again.

Fuck, me, she is incredible.

As she draws the light back into herself, absorbing the prisoners' anguish, my heart pounds in my chest. The sheer magnitude of her power is astounding.

Not because of what she is doing right now – although, admittedly, doing it for twenty people is a feat most empaths would balk at – but because she is doing it so easily. After two hundred years of *not* doing anything at all.

When she is thrown back against the wall, her body racked with pain, my knuckles whiten with the force of my clenched fists. She cannot break. Not now.

Not before I have truly understood what she is.

And what she means to my kingdom.

Chapter Twenty-Six

ALANA

*T*WO WEEKS LATER

FOR TWO WEEKS I HEAR NOTHING FROM ELDRION, AND I am not permitted to leave my chamber.

All day I simply watch out of the window as the citadel brightens with the sun and darkens with the moon. Even Finn does not come to see me. Briony tells me he's too afraid, that the entire castle is on lockdown and terrified of Eldrion's dark, festering mood.

Last night, I plucked up the nerve to ask her what happened to Kayan's body.

She told me she didn't know, but I'm not sure that I believe her.

I asked how the others were and, again, she said she did not know. Now that Henrik is gone, she has no contact down in the cells. And this makes me realise how much harder it's going to be for me to get access to the others in order to help them.

Despite what happened to Kayan – perhaps *because* of what happened to him – I am still determined to help them.

For two weeks, I have thought of little else.

When I first arrived, I told myself I had no magic that would be useful in an escape attempt. If I did, why would Eldrion let me walk free?

But what if I was wrong?

I was able to take the grief of twenty people – twenty – and ease it without meaning to.

One hundred years ago, though, I took more than that from Kayan.

What if I learned to take people's minds, stop their thoughts, steal their thoughts, make it so they cannot chase us?

What if I can do more than absorb feelings?

What if I can manipulate them? Make people trust me? Make them open the cells, open the doors, let us run free?

I don't for a moment think I could control Eldrion this way.

I still have no true understanding of what his powers are. But I know he is stronger than the entire city of Luminael put together. If I could do it quickly, though, and do it while he is distracted, perhaps there would be a chance.

Outside, it is getting darker.

As has become custom at sunset, Briony enters the room with a tray of food and a glass of wine. She sets them down on the table, goes to the stone bench in front of the fire, and sits down.

Since Henrik's death, she has not been herself.

"He wants to see you tonight," she says, looking down at her clasped hands instead of at me.

"Is there to be a feast?" I ask.

"Yes," she replies, her voice willowy and weak.

"Has he specified what I should wear?"

"No," she says again, "just that you're to come to him when the feast is done."

"I'm not hungry."

I walk past the tray, reach for my gloves, and then decide to leave them where they are. Even Briony does not seem to care anymore whether I wear them or not.

"Do you need to accompany me?" I ask. She nods, then follows behind me as I walk through the castle towards the Grand Hall. When we reach his doors, I pause and turn to her. "Briony, are we still friends?"

She meets my eyes, and she looks as though she's fighting the urge to cry.

"Yes, of course. I just thought . . ." She hesitates. "I didn't think you would want to be my friend anymore."

"Why?" I ask, frowning.

Again, she clasps her hands together, worrying them in front of her stomach. "Because it was me who told Eldrion what was happening in the dungeon. If I hadn't —" she pinches the bridge of her nose like she's trying to physically keep the tears inside her body.

"I don't blame you for that." I reach out and take her hand, squeezing it tightly even though I'm not wearing my gloves. She doesn't seem to care.

"I heard the commotion. I heard them saying Henrik was dead. I didn't even think about what Eldrion would do to them. I just . . ."

"You were scared." I squeeze her hand again. "I do not blame you. And I absolutely still want to be your friend."

She smiles, and for the first time since we have known each other, I hug her tightly. Then I turn, take a deep breath, and push open the doors.

I EXPECT THE ATMOSPHERE IN THE HALL TO BE DIFFERENT. I expect it to be sombre or melancholy, but it is as if the Sunborne of the citadel have forgotten what happened on the parapet two weeks ago, as if they have forgotten Kayan completely.

As I have every other night when I've been forced to attend these evenings, I filter through the crowd so I can see Finn when he performs.

After two weeks, I am desperate to see him, but when he appears, I instantly know there is something wrong.

I follow his gaze. He is staring at something in the corner of the room that no one else seems to have noticed. The drums start sooner than usual, and something moves in the shadows.

Two sprawling black wings appear, and then there he is . . . Eldrion.

An audible gasp spreads through the hall as Eldrion strides into the spotlight.

He stands beside Finn and holds out his hand. Tentatively, Finn places the ribbon into it. The one that is usually used by a woman in the audience to bind him.

I have not seen him perform this part of his dance since he gave himself to me and taught me how to use the rope to pin his wings to his chest.

I was worried about how I would feel seeing another woman do this to him. But Eldrion doing it?

I glance at Briony. "What's happening?"

She does not reply, but she looks terrified, and so does Finn.

Very slowly, Eldrion begins to circle Finn, holding the ribbon taut in his hands. Without speaking, he plays the part that a Sunborne woman normally plays. He binds Finn's wings tight to his chest, all while the drumbeat matches the pounding rhythm of my heart.

When I did this for Finn, it was a mark of control but I was not rough or cruel. Eldrion, however, revels in his power.

He fastens the ribbons tightly. They press into Finn's wings and make him wince. Behind his mask, his eyes are dark and swimming with humiliation.

When Eldrion has finished, he stands back and stretches out his arms proudly.

"Now let us see if the jester can escape my knots," he says, moving into the crowd as a wave of applause breaks out, and a few women visibly swoon as Eldrion flexes his muscles.

I stare at Finn, willing him to have the strength to break free, but he doesn't look at me. Shame hums on his skin as he strains against Eldrion's bindings. They are too tight. He will never break free of them. And that is the point, isn't it? That is what Eldrion is trying to show everyone.

The display on the parapet wasn't enough. He needs to hammer it home just a little bit more.

No one escapes the citadel.

No one.

I reach for Briony's hand, and we hold on to each other as Eldrion commands that the jester try harder, and Finn squirms and writhes.

The scene continues to unfold for more minutes than I can count. It feels like a lifetime. I want to run to him and untie him and take him away from this place, but I can't. I want to take his pain away, but I can't do that either because everyone else would see my light.

I can do nothing but watch.

Finally, as the crowd begins to grow bored of the display, Eldrion strides back into the centre of the room, takes a knife from his belt, the same knife he used to slit Kayan's throat, and cuts the ribbons away from Finn.

The knife nicks Finn's wing, and the piercings on their tips jingle sadly.

He stumbles back, trying to regain his composure, but Eldrion towers above him, holding the broken ribbons, his eyes boring into Finn's as if he is saying, *Now you know. Now you know that you can never be free of me.*

Chapter Twenty-Seven

ALANA

*M*y eyes blur with tears. I cannot wait any longer. For the first time since I've been here, the Sunborne are watching me. Looking for me to react, as if they are enjoying the cruelty that has tugged emotion from my body.

Taking my hand, Briony whispers, "Come with me," and drags me away through the crowd.

At the back of the hall, we take a corridor I haven't travelled before and keep going until we reach a small wooden door. Briony lifts the latch, pushes it open, and we emerge onto a small cobbled path that leads across a grassy lawn.

When we reach a row of dishevelled hedging, we pass through a gap in its middle, and I inhale sharply at the sight of a small, sparkling lake.

"I had no idea this was here," I whisper.

Briony puts her hand on my lower back. "Eldrion used to

come here a lot," she says. "Now he spends most of his days locked in his chambers."

At the thought of Eldrion's chambers, I shudder.

I've been trying not to think about what I witnessed there, and what I did there – what I was doing while Kayan was dying. As the memory takes over, another sob shakes my shoulders, and Briony urges me down the slope towards the water.

When we reach it, out here in the moonlight, away from the castle, I feel like I can breathe for the first time in weeks.

I brace my hands on my hips, bend over, and breathe deeply.

Then I begin to pace up and down, shaking my arms and my wings, trying to relieve the tension that seems to be overwhelming my entire body.

"I can't close my eyes," I tell her. "All I can see is Kayan."

Briony doesn't reply, just stands there. A stoic presence, watching over me.

"Why would he do that to Finn?" I stop, anger bubbling up hotter than my sadness as thoughts of Kayan and Finn tussle with each other in my head.

"Because that's what he does," Briony says. "He humiliates, and he tortures, and he kills, and he is cruel. And that is how he keeps us under his control." Her jaw twitches. She hesitates, as if she's about to say something.

"Go on," I tell her. "You don't need to hide anything from me, Briony. What were you about to say?"

Wrapping her arms around her waist, she walks to the edge of the lake and looks out over the water. It is small and not as beautiful as the lakes at home, but it is still beautiful compared to the cold stone walls of the castle. So, I stand beside her and wait until she's ready to speak.

"Kayan challenged Henrik once on why he was helping Eldrion. I think he believed the Shadowkind should rise up and fight back. But it's not that easy."

She doesn't look at me, just keeps staring out, her eyes fixated on a spot on the horizon.

"He and his family have spent centuries perfecting how to keep us under control. What happened with Kayan? That's nothing compared to what he's done to others. What he did to Finn, that was a second warning. That was to let us know we are still his." She shrugs, a small sigh biting her lips. "And we will be his forever."

I breathe out hard, rubbing my hands, rubbing my palms over my face. My hair is tied back and suddenly it feels too tight, too restrained, so I pull it loose and shake it over my shoulders.

"I saw something in Eldrion's chambers," I speak quietly, almost hoping that Briony won't hear me.

But this time, she turns towards me, and her eyebrows quirk with interest. "What did you see?" she asks.

I shake my head. Shame scratches beneath my skin. "I walked in on him . . ."

I cast my eyes down towards Briony's pelvis in the hopes she might understand what I'm trying to say. "Saw him . . . walked . . . I walked in on him. He was naked. There was a huge, shimmering image in the middle of the room, an image of me and him together." I hesitate. "Fucking. And he was . . ."

Briony's eyes widen. "What did it look like?"

I blush as the image of me and Eldrion reappears in my mind.

"I mean, was it cast in the air? Was it in a pool of water?"

"It was in the air. It appeared like a window or picture, just shimmering there in front of him."

"Did he say anything before it appeared?"

I shake my head. "I didn't even know it was possible to do that, to create visions and . . ."

Briony bites her lip thoughtfully.

"What is it?"

When she looks back at me, she reaches for my hand and squeezes it tightly. "You mustn't feel guilty," she says.

"You don't know the worst bit." I lace my fingers together and squeeze tightly, my knuckles whitening with the pressure. "I liked it . . . No, I didn't like it, but it made me feel . . ."

The blush intensifies and my mouth goes dry. I can't believe I'm saying this out loud, but I need to say it to someone.

"While Kayan was dying, that's what I was doing." Finally, the shame gives way to heartbreak, and my voice cracks because I start to cry again.

Briony squeezes my elbow, then walks towards a small bramble of bushes nearby. When she returns, she's holding a rose. Picking off the thorns, she puts it into my hand and tells me to inhale the scent slowly. I do what she says and immediately begin to feel calmer.

But when I open my eyes and look at the petals, I don't see pale, delicate pink. I see ice. A memory barrels into me so unexpectedly that I can barely stay standing, but I try to push through it. Try to find the happiness because I know it's there somewhere.

I feel my lips part into a smile.

"Better?" Briony asks.

I nod and tell her the story of Kayan and me by the lake. The day he showed me how he learned to control his powers and create ice from water.

"It wasn't long before . . ." I hesitate.

"The accident," Briony finishes.

I nod, brushing my fingers across the rose petals. "Before that, we used to meet at the lake all the time. It was our place. We would skip stones, and he was always so angry that I was better at it than him. That night, the night with the rose, he cheated. He used his powers to help it skip all the way to the other side. And he thought he was so clever and so funny." I start to laugh.

Briony smiles too, then she moves away from me slightly, looks down towards her feet, and stoops to pick up two pebbles. "It must be hard not having a body," she says. "At least I've been able to say goodbye to Henrik properly."

I nod, tears pricking my eyes again.

"So, let's say something for him now." She passes me one of the pebbles. "Let's skip some stones and share some memories of Kayan and say goodbye. And then maybe you'll feel stronger."

I rub my thumb over the pebble. Gratitude swells in my chest. "Thank you," I say.

Turning towards the water, Briony skips her stone first, sharing a memory of Kayan being gentle and kind and always looking after the people in the cells.

I look down at my pebble and try to remember how I used to do this. It has been over one hundred years. Yet, the movement still feels familiar. With a flick of my wrist, I skip the stone across the lake surface. It creates ripples, making the exact pattern I expect it to make. And suddenly, in the centre of the lake, it drops, leaving one large ripple making a strange, undulating pattern across the surface.

As I watch it, a surge of energy courses through my body. It is completely unfamiliar and feels like nothing I can name. It's like light and energy swelling inside me. And then I remember what Kayan said when he told me that his powers were different from mine. How he could feel them, how he latched onto them without really knowing how.

I try to catch hold of the feeling and focus on it. As I do, the ripples turn into a swirl. They move faster and faster, then begin to skip up into the air, droplets forming delicate, intricate patterns.

I glance at Briony. She is watching me in awe, eyes wide, her hands shaking.

But I'm not shaking. I've never felt more alive as a shimmering display of water and light materialises above the lake. "What's happening?" Briony asks. "You said you didn't have any magic . . ."

I don't even need to think before answering her. The word is on my lips within a heartbeat. "Kayan," I whisper. "It's Kayan's power."

I glance at her again. "Perhaps I had it all along."

Chapter Twenty-Eight

ALANA

*W*hen we arrive at Finn's room, my knuckles rap urgently against the weathered wood of his door. It takes every bit of willpower I have not to scream for him to answer me.

The sound swells in the air.

A moment passes, in which I can barely breathe. I need to tell him what happened. I need to *show* him what happened.

Finally, the latch clicks and the door swings inwards with a creak.

"Alana . . ." Finn breathes my name like a prayer, ushering me inside. It has been too long since we saw each other, and the need to be close to him is so strong I can hardly stand it.

He is uneasy, and ashamed, and I cannot bear to have him feeling this way.

As my eyes adjust to the darkness, I notice the way he is standing – beside the wall, gaze cast down towards his feet. Tendrils of embarrassment snake through the air around him. His wings, so delicate compared to Lord Eldrion's, twitch nervously at his back.

"It's not much," he says, looking around his chamber.

"I don't care." I move to take his hands but then I change my mind. "Something happened."

He tilts his head, examining the way I'm standing. "What is it?" Concern softens his eyes.

I hesitate. Suddenly, telling him doesn't feel right. Not when he's like this . . . Humiliated and broken by Eldrion's display.

Smoothing my palms over his chest, I move them to his neck, up to his face, and stroke from his chin up towards his ears. He leans into my touch and closes his eyes. "I can tell you later," I whisper. "For now, I want to take away the hurt."

Finn presses his forehead to mine. "I'll be all right," he mutters.

But I stand back, drop my arms to my sides, and drop my gaze to my feet. "I'm yours, Finn." I stand completely motionless. "Do what you want with me."

Finn stares at me for a moment. His tongue moistens his lower lip, and he inhales deeply. The muscles in his jaw twitch. His gaze has darkened. "Alana . . ."

"I want to help you the way you helped me, but you don't need me to take away your feelings. You need me to give you something back." I tilt my chin up, presenting myself to him. "I know what it's like to need to seize control."

Breathing heavily, anticipation shimmers in the air between us.

Finn draws closer. Now, his eyes gleam with something untamed. Something feral. Something that makes my skin prickle and my breath quicken.

And it is not just his gaze that has changed; the air has changed, too. All around him, I feel longing, lust, and an edge of adrenaline. It is the adrenaline that excites me the most – his desire to take back what Eldrion just took from him.

"You are sure?" he asks, trailing an index finger across my collarbone.

My response is a breathless sound, barely audible over the blood rushing in my ears. I close my eyes and let his newfound dominance wash over me.

Finn nods slowly, then unfastens his mask and sets it down on the mantel above the fire. I smile when I see his face, but the look in his eyes takes my smile and turns it into breathy, open-mouthed anticipation.

"Strip," he commands. "Stand here. Hands flat on the stone, legs apart, facing the wall."

I hesitate for the span of a heartbeat before complying, peeling away layers of silk and leather, feeling the cool kiss of the air on my skin. My wings tremble with anticipation. My entire body craves his touch.

Beneath my fingertips, the wall is rough and cold. I press my palms flat against it, aware only of the sound of my own breath and the faint flicker of candlelight casting dancing shadows.

Finn moves behind me, the subtle chime of bells announcing the presence of his wings. Then he brings something to my face. A blindfold. He pulls it tight over my eyes and fastens it gently. "Can you see?" he asks.

I shake my head. "No. I cannot."

"Retract your wings."

I hesitate. I thought he was going to tie me up. I pictured him looping the rope between my breasts, binding my wings tightly, then fucking me while I cannot move.

"I said, retract them." He gives my left wing a sharp tug that causes me to moan with both pleasure and pain. When I do as he asks, he whispers, "Good girl," then slides his hand between my thighs and cups my pussy. Applying pressure – hard but not moving – he blows warm air on my neck, then grazes my flesh with his teeth.

I flex my fingers, scraping the stone with my nails.

"Don't move. Unless it becomes too much."

I swallow hard. The power emanating from Finn's body and mind seeps into my skin and turns to liquid heat in my core.

He steps away from me. I hear him removing his clothes, then feel him draw closer once more.

With my sight removed, everything feels heightened.

His back meets mine. I wait for him to turn around so his cock is pressed against my ass, but he doesn't.

If he's not going to fuck me from behind, what in the stars is he going to do to me?

For the longest time, he doesn't move. His presence becomes a column of heat. And then I feel his wings emerge. At first, they caress my back, fluttering gently. A pang of sympathy swells in my chest because I know how badly he wishes they were bigger, bolder, stronger.

But then their pace changes.

He is beating them harder.

The gentle stroking begins to sting. I wince, but he beats harder still.

And harder.

And harder.

The motion sends whip-like ripples through the air, each stroke needling my exposed flesh. Notes of pleasure and pain rise from the core of my being. I give in to the pain. I slam my hands against the wall but do not move.

I can take it.

I want him to know I can take it.

"Finn . . ."

He stops for a quivering, pulsating second, but does not answer me.

Panting, I rest my forehead on the wall. My back burns. Pain radiates down over my ass to the tops of my thighs. My legs tremble.

There is a heavy pause. Finn releases a guttural roar. I expect to feel the thrum of his wings on my flesh but, instead, his hands are on my hips. He pulls the blindfold from my eyes, spins me around, and strokes my face.

Pressed against the cold stone wall, my back sighs with relief. "You took them so well," he whispers.

All I can do is nod, and hook my legs around his waist as he lifts me onto his cock.

He thrusts upwards. I grip his shoulders, then release my wings. As they push through my sore skin, I cry out but then I beat them gently, using them to keep me suspended in the air so he can fuck me while I kiss him and stroke him and moan into his mouth.

When he comes, he grabs my ass and I let his orgasm wash over me, coaxing mine through the haze of pain and pleasure to swell in the deepest crevices of my body.

For a long time, we remain suspended in the middle of the room. Slowly, my wings calm, and Finn lifts me down. I lean against his chest, shaking. And when he tucks his finger beneath my chin and turns my face up towards him, I hear myself whisper, "I love you, Finn."

He stares down at me. His beautiful features are emphasised by the glow of the candles. "I love you too."

Chapter Twenty-Nine

ALANA

*W*hen I finally leave Finn and go to Eldrion, I find him stalking back and forth like a caged animal. His usually perfect hair is tousled, his muscles tight, and there is an almost-empty bottle of whisky on the mantlepiece above the fire.

He looks at me and daggers nestle between my ribs and my stomach. He might have trusted me once, but not anymore. Now, all I see when I look at him is pure, molten, hatred.

Hatred and the sting of Finn's lashings on my back.

I take my eyes away from him, staring down at my bare feet. In my mind, I hear those sounds again. The tearing of Kayan's wings, the scream, the thud. I see Finn, and the way he looked when Eldrion humiliated him.

"You are late." He flexes his fingers.

He pours himself another drink and sighs as if he is in physical pain. When I look up, he is rubbing his temples.

"I will not be discussing anything else with you." I sit down in his armchair, cross one leg over the other, and fold my arms in front of my stomach. It is taking every ounce of strength in my body not to crumble, sob, run. But I will not let him see I am scared of him. "You can keep making me come here, but from now on I have nothing to say to you."

I am trying to breathe slowly, trying to trick my nervous system into believing everything is okay, when he strides across the room to stand in front of me. His enormous frame casts a dark shadow over my face. I keep my gaze trained on my intertwined fingers.

But then his hand is on my chin and he is jerking my face up towards his.

I jolt back in the chair. I see him grabbing Kayan, lifting him into the air with one hand. Nausea surges at the back of my throat. I stand, pushing past him, and vomit onto the floor beneath the window.

Eldrion simply watches me.

I brace my hand on the window, letting the cool glass soothe my palm, and breathe heavily. Then I wipe my mouth with the back of my hand, and straighten myself.

Eldrion assesses me for a moment, then hands me the whisky.

I take it and drink it down in one, wincing as it burns on its way down my throat.

"You took away their pain," he says slowly. He's talking about the cells.

I open my mouth to talk, then stop myself. I vowed not to speak, and I won't.

"It was magnificent." His eyes change. Something in them softens, but then he seems to notice it and quickly corrects himself. Looking down at the remnants of my breakfast, which now stain his floor, he takes my wrist and jerks me away from them.

He is so strong, his grip so powerful, I could not refuse him even if I tried. He drags me over to the fireplace, then pours me another drink. The last of his whisky.

"You are very powerful," he says.

I shudder because it feels more like an insult than a compliment.

"But you have no idea how dangerous your powers are."

My grip tightens on my glass, nails scratching the smooth surface. "Dangerous to you?" Damn it, if he wants to talk, then we'll talk. But I am not going to be the one giving answers today; *he* is.

"Not to me," he says. "To everything."

"You are speaking in riddles. Either tell me what you want from me or let me go."

Eldrion's lips curl into a vicious smile. "Let you go?" he laughs, tipping back his head. "You think I would let you go now?"

I stare at him defiantly, struck by the sudden knowledge that I no longer have anything to lose. Except my life. And if Kayan lost his, why should mine be any more precious? "Tell me what you want from me," I spit.

"I will not tell you that." Eldrion steeples his fingers. "But I will tell you that you were right. I found you long before I paid for you."

My eyes flash and I swallow forcefully. "Why?"

"I heard rumours of an empath living amongst the Leaf-borne. I wanted to find out if it was true."

"You came to my village?" I take in his vast wings and shake my head. "I think we would have noticed you."

"Not me." Eldrion meets my eyes. Something flickers in his icy gaze. "Finn."

A laugh stutters on my lips. I shake my head.

"Finn tracked you down for me. He was supposed to capture you on the night of the centennial, but the Gloomweavers put pay to our plan."

My legs feel as if they have turned to liquid. I grip onto the mantlepiece to steady myself, and memories of all the ways I have given myself to the jester swim behind my eyes.

My back burns.

I trusted him. I let him . . .

Shaking my head, I screw my eyes closed and try to make sense of what Eldrion is saying to me. "Finn?" I mutter.

When I look at Eldrion again, he is smirking. A vicious smirk that tells me he knows what Finn means to me and he waited until this very second to reveal the truth about him.

"Search my emotions," he says, leaning back, pushing back his shoulders, opening his chest as though he expects me to slam my hands onto him and scour his body for traces of a lie.

"I do not want to be anywhere near *your* emotions." I flex

my fingers, put down the whisky, pick it back up again and drink it in one.

"Then ask him yourself." Eldrion leans back and gestures to the door. "I'm sure you won't mind getting close to *his* emotions."

Chapter Thirty

ALANA

"*I*t was you . . ." I throw open Finn's door and stride into the room.

He sits up and scrambles out of bed.

"Eldrion sent you to watch me." My chest tightens, and I have no idea if it is because I am feeling Finn's panic or my own. "He sent you to *take* me."

I start to pace up and down, shaking my head.

I wait for Finn to object. To tell me I'm wrong. But he doesn't, and when I look at him again I know that everything Eldrion told me was the truth.

Anger dissolves into my muscles and turns them weak. I sit down hard in the chair by the fire. "You lied to me."

Finn holds up his hands, palms out, like I'm a frightened animal about to flee. "Alana, please. Let me explain."

"I trusted you." Tears escape and roll down my cheeks.

"You can still trust me. Please, let me —"

I feel completely exposed. He has seen every part of me – my body and my soul. And I thought I had seen every part of him. But, this entire time, he has been lying to me. "Was it all fake? Were you just using me because Eldrion told you to? Trying to get close to me? Manipulate me?"

Finn sighs loudly and shakes his head. "Alana, I can explain if you'll let me."

The anger is back. Fury begins to gnaw at my bones. I stand and put my hands on my hips, ignoring the tug of pain the movement draws from my back because it is still stinging with the memory of his wings. "Then explain . . ."

"Eldrion did send me to watch you. That's true."

Hearing him say the words out loud forces the breath from my lungs. I clutch at my chest and then try to regain some sense of composure.

If he has lied to me all this time, if he doesn't truly love me, and if everything was fake, I will not give him the satisfaction of seeing me crumble.

"How long?" I ask.

Finn presses his lips together as if he is battling the urge to answer my question, knowing that when he does, everything will change.

"Since the last centennial," he says, looking down at his feet. I almost laugh because it is so ridiculous.

"One hundred years." The words taste like lies on my tongue. "You have been watching me in secret for one hundred years?"

Finn gives a small shrug that makes me almost wild with rage, as if it's perfectly understandable, as if it's nothing outrageous, as if one hundred years go by in the blink of an eye, and who can blame him for not telling me?

"Not all the time," he says. "Once we found you, I came every few years, gave him updates. That's all."

"Updates on what?"

"I didn't really know," Finn says, "and that's the truth. You can search my mind, and you'll see."

"I don't want to search your mind. I don't want to know anything about your mind," I snap.

Finn reaches for me and then stops, as if he knows that is the last thing I want.

"He didn't tell me why, I swear. Just that there was a girl who was special and that I was to find her, keep watch over her, and then . . ."

"Kidnap her." I step closer, looking straight up into his eyes, hoping that he sees defiance in mine.

"He didn't tell me that part until —" Finn pinches the bridge of his nose.

For the first time since I saw him without his mask, I wish he would put it back on because right now, I do not want to be looking at his face.

"Did he also tell you to fuck me?" I ask, and now I can't hold back the tears anymore. They roll down my cheeks treacherously, and when Finn folds me into his embrace, I want to fight him, but I don't.

"No, he didn't tell me to fall in love with you either."

I shake my head and try to pull away, but he holds me still.

"I fell in love with you, Alana. I loved you before I'd ever spoken to you."

"And yet, you would have given me to him anyway."

Finn steps back, rubbing his upper arms. His wings droop a little, and those chimes that used to send trickles of arousal to my core now only send sadness to my heart. "I had no choice," he says.

"There is always a choice," I snap back. "What else haven't you told me?"

"Nothing," he says. "I swear it."

He takes my hands and presses them to his chest. "Please, search my mind so you know I'm telling you the truth."

"I shouldn't have to," I breathe, snapping my hand back and wiping the tears from my cheeks. But I do it anyway.

I let my powers free, and I let his feelings engulf me.

"What else haven't you told me?" I ask again.

When he replies, "Nothing," I know he's telling me the truth, and it doesn't feel like enough.

Chapter Thirty-One

FINN

*S*he is panicking, pulling away from me. I don't need to be an empath to see the walls slamming down in front of her right now.

Despite her anger, she is beautiful. Maybe even more beautiful like this. Raw, sweat-laced skin, flushed cheeks, and fury in her eyes.

"You should have *told* me."

"How could I?" I slide my hand around to her back and gently caress the fabric that hides imprints left by the sting of my wings. "I would have lost you." I slot my other hand into hers and lace our fingers together. I stare into her eyes, trying to make her see the sincerity in my words. "It's because of me that you're here. How could I tell you that?"

Alana lets go of my hand and paces away from me. She shakes her head, her auburn hair falling over her shoulders, and her wings flutter so hard they whip air across my face. She is so beautiful I want to devour her.

Even more beautiful when her face is etched with anger, power, fury.

Without breaking eye contact, I drop to my knees in front of her.

She presses her lips together, and her eyes widen. She loves it when I kneel like this.

"That's why you've given yourself to me the way you have," she says, her voice strong instead of quiet. "To ease your guilt?"

I hang my head, bracing my hands on my knees. "I wanted to help you see what I see. I wanted to help you take control." In a whisper, I add, "It was the least I could do."

There is a long, quivering pause, and then she pads softly towards me. Bending down, she grabs hold of my hair and roughly jerks my face up towards her. Without breaking eye contact, she takes hold of my mask, rips it from my face and tosses it across the room. Then she strides to the chest at the bottom of the bed and takes out the rope.

Anticipation burns inside me, and my cock hardens.

Watching her stroll towards me, rope in her hands, and that look in her eyes – like she wants to completely destroy me – brings saliva to my mouth and tension to my balls.

Her movements are fluid, her hands deftly working the rope as she binds my hands and feet. The fibres are rough against my skin as she fastens my hands tightly behind my back.

I expect her to straddle my face and make me lick her pussy. Instead, she grabs my head, jerks my hair back, gives my cheek a light slap, then pushes me forward so I'm bent double, chest pressed against the floor.

"Should I retract my wings?" I stutter.

She doesn't answer, just walks over to the table next to the bed and picks up my water jug. "I have something to show you," she says. "I'm still practicing but . . ." Waving one hand over the jug, her eyes shimmer as the water levitates into the air and starts to swirl – a beautiful, suspended whirlpool flickering in the candlelight.

I start to sit up, but she shakes her head at me.

"Would you like to see it?"

I nod. She can do magic? The pieces immediately slot into place. Water magic. Kayan's magic. Her grief must have –

"I asked if you'd like to see?" she snaps.

"Yes. Show me."

She smiles, puts the jug back down, then blows across her palms. As her breath meets the whirlpool, it changes shape, crackles, and solidifies into a large, rounded icicle. Hanging in the air. Brilliant white, so cold I can almost feel it from here.

Walking slowly back to me, she holds the icicle in her hands. The look in her eyes tells me to stay exactly where I am.

Crouching down, spreading her legs so I can see her cunt, she slips a finger into my mouth, opens it, then inserts the icicle. "Suck," she whispers.

A jolt of pure, molten arousal goes straight to my cock as I do as she commands. She smiles at me, then dips a hand between her thighs and closes her eyes while she touches herself.

When she opens them again, she stands up, freeing my mouth, then walks slowly around me. Dragging the shaft of ice down my spine, she blows warm air on the trail it leaves, sending sparks of arousal cascading through me.

When she reaches the top of my ass, I tense.

Without speaking, she parts my legs, and the stretch of my thighs jerks a sigh from my lips.

Another breath of warm air, and then she begins to tease my tight hole with the tip of the shaft. I flinch at the sensation – cold and unexpected, and the more I tense, the more I'm aware I need to *un*tense.

But then a small fizz of anticipation begins to build, and I realise I am leaning back towards her, searching for more pressure. She senses it too – of course, she does. She knows exactly what I want because, at this moment, I am not trying to hide anything from her.

She takes hold of my hip, biting into it with her fingernails. She starts to ease in the shaft. Then, with a suddenness that steals my breath, she presses it inside me, slowly but inexorably filling me with a pleasure so intense it borders on pain.

I gasp as my body tries to adjust to what is happening, and Alana sighs loudly.

I crane my head, desperate to see the look on her face, but she snaps at me to keep looking at the floor. The timbre of her voice – sharp and commanding – makes me moan.

For a moment, she just holds me still and waits for my body to adjust to the fullness. Then, slowly, she starts to move it.

My eyes roll back and I scrape the concrete floor with my nails. "Fuck, Alana . . ."

She hesitates, worried she's hurting me, but I shake my head and plead with her.

"Don't stop . . . Fuck me harder."

I can almost feel her smiling as she does as I ask, and while she starts to thrust, I strain against the ties on my wrists, desperate to wrap my hand around my cock.

Sensing what I need, Alana reaches between my spread-open legs and curls her firm fingers around my length. Her movements are rhythmic and deliberate, and my body feels like it's being burned alive from the inside out. Pleasure and pain collide, my thoughts disappear, everything is dark and loud, and there is nothing but *feeling*.

Just when I think I can't bear anymore, she quickens the pace.

She lets go of my cock and the sound she makes tells me she's started to fuck herself while she fucks me. I arch my back, unable to resist the force of her movements. Her wings flutter above us, casting dark shadows on the walls. She is moaning loudly. I can feel her power flowing through me. It surges through my veins, filling every fibre of my being. And it feels like . . . magic.

Until this second, magic has existed as only a flicker inside me. Deep in the shadowy basement of my soul. Forgotten, repressed, contained.

But it's not my magic I'm feeling. This is different. It's pure, and big, and powerful. So fucking powerful.

My eyes spring open.

Alana cries out. She thrusts deeper, harder, and the magic is drowned out by the sound of my orgasm. It reverberates in my chest, vibrating through my bones. I can feel it in every cell, every atom of my body. The force of her power, the intensity of her control, coalesces into a single, over-whelming sensation.

It builds deep inside me and then explodes in waves.

When she unties me and slips her hands under my arms, helping me to my feet, she stares into my eyes and smiles.

"Did you feel that?" I breathe, panting.

"Did I hurt you?" she replies.

I shake my head, trying to read her face. She didn't feel what I felt. She didn't feel her magic seeping into my bones. She has no idea what just happened, and I have no idea *how* it happened.

All I know is that I want to feel it again.

I *need* to feel it again.

I need her.

All of her.

"Do you think it was Kayan's magic?" I ask gently, arm draped around her shoulders.

"I don't know." Her reply is tight and restrained. She doesn't trust me anymore. I broke it, which means I need to fix it and fast.

"Alana, I'm sorry I lied. I will do anything to make it up to you."

I stroke her shoulder and kiss her forehead. Despite what just happened between us, I still feel as if she is turning away from me.

And now more than ever, I know I need to bring her back.

"You can't make it up to me, Finn. You can hammer nails into a fence but when you take the nails out, the holes are still there."

I think about her words and the meaning solidifies like iron in my gut. "If I broke us, I'll never forgive myself."

Sitting up, she reaches for a glass of water, takes a sip and then pinches the bridge of her nose as if she's trying to think. "I still want to free the others," she says. "If you want to make it up to me, if you want to start making it up to me, you'll help me figure out how to do that."

I inhale sharply and accept the glass from her, taking a long drink of my own. "Alana, I know exactly how," I say, my voice filled with conviction. "But you have to trust me."

She frowns at me. "What do you mean?"

I stand up and extend my hand to her. "Get dressed. There's something I need to show you."

ALANA DRESSES IN SILENCE. SHE IS LOST IN THOUGHT, BUT I know as soon as she sees the whole picture, she will forget what Eldrion told her. She'll forget my lies, and understand why I had to do it.

I lead her out of the room and we navigate through the castle's winding corridors until we reach the kitchens.

The sights and noises, Shadowkind still clearing up after the banquet, are overwhelming. Alana blinks at the clattering of pots and pans, but I keep hold of her hand and lead her towards the back.

When we reach the pantry, I usher her inside and close the door behind us. It is cool in here, and dark. In the corner, there is a pile of old grain sacks. I tug them aside to reveal a concealed hatch in the floor.

"What is that?" Alana tilts her head.

I tap on the hatch with my foot, three times, quick succession. Then I lift it open.

Alana peers down into the darkness of the opening.

"Ladies first." I hold out my hand. Alana hesitates, but then visibly pushes back her shoulders, swipes her hair back and ties it at the base of her neck. Swinging herself down onto the top rail of the dark staircase, she disappears.

This is it.

The moment Alana Leafborne joins the fight.

Chapter Thirty-Two

ALANA

I shouldn't trust him. He lied to me. Worse than that; he worked *with* Eldrion.

I know these things, and yet I also know that when I'm with him I do not feel even the slightest flicker of malice. When I'm around Eldrion, my entire body reacts to him. I feel the evil seeping from his pores even with my gates slammed shut.

Finn has never made me feel that way.

So, I follow him when he leads me to a secret trapdoor at the back of the kitchens.

We descend into the darkness beneath the door, taking shaky steps down, down, down until it becomes pitch-dark.

But then there is light again. Flickering torchlight.

My feet meet with solid ground. Not stone, but soil, compacted. It smells damp here. Like earth, and life, and home. Thoughts of the Leafborne forests flood into my mind, but they disappear abruptly when the flickering candlelight illuminates several faces in the dark.

I recognise Briony at once and rush to her side. She embraces me tightly, and I feel like she simply isn't going to let go of me. When she does, I see more faces. Some of them I recognise. Some I don't. All are clearly Shadowkind, dressed in uniform that shows they work in some capacity for Eldrion.

"What is she doing here?" someone hisses loudly.

Briony shakes her head. "I don't know. Wait for Finn. I can hear him."

A moment later, Finn drops to the ground and immediately whips off his mask. Throwing it to the floor, he claps his hands. "It's time," he says enigmatically.

When the others exchange worried glances, I take his elbow and gesture to our surroundings. "What is this place, Finn?"

Finn inhales deeply, then puts his hands on my forearms and looks down into my eyes. His are warm and dark, and for the longest moment I just stare into them wishing we could go back to that night in the forest. Wishing he'd told me what he was doing there. Wishing he'd asked me to run away with him because I would have, in a heartbeat, even though we didn't know each other then.

"It's our way out." His answer hangs in the air. The silence swells.

"We always knew we wouldn't be able to escape Eldrion quickly. With some unplanned, hurried attack on the castle. He has spies even within the Shadowkind. Not all of us can be trusted."

My stomach tenses. "Who would want to be a spy for him?"

Interjecting, Briony says, "He blackmails, uses people's families against them. He's clever, and cruel, and not all of us are strong enough to withstand what he dishes out."

The others nod in agreement, and Finn continues, "So, we played the long game. Yarrow's father started it." He gestures to a tall, grey-bearded guard who is standing with his arms folded in front of his chest. "And Yarrow is the only one left now of the original rebels. We are all second generation."

"Rebels?" I almost laugh, even though it's not funny. Then realise it's a spark of hope that has ignited my laughter.

While Yarrow stares at me unblinkingly, Finn nods. "This tunnel," he says, "leads to another, and another. A rabbit warren of them. All exiting in different places beyond the citadel."

"They go under the ocean?"

"Deep under," he replies. "The rebels have spent two hundred years digging these tunnels, Alana. Bit by bit, every night, in snippets of time, we have made our escape route. They have been ready for years, but we have been waiting for the right moment."

"It has been a long wait," Briony sighs.

"But with your magic, Alana, we finally have it."

"My magic?"

In a gruff timbre, Yarrow barks, "Briony says you have water magic?" He glances at my wrists. "Yet you are not cuffed like the others."

"Eldrion doesn't know." I look down at my hands. "I didn't even know until tonight."

"Show us." Yarrow nods at my hands. "I want to see for myself. We've waited too long to take risks."

Grasping my hands, Finn says, "Will you?"

My brow furrows with worry. "I haven't had a chance to hone or practice my magic. I don't know . . ."

"You don't need to practice, Alana. You have Kayan's magic. It is as established in you as it was in him." He clears his throat and rubs the back of his neck. "At least, from what I've seen, that's my guess."

I start to blush but then someone at the back reminds us we don't have much time before sunrise, so I close my eyes, focus on the scent of the damp soil beneath my feet, and stretch out my hands. Slowly, droplets of water start to filter up into the air.

Yarrow's eyes widen. A few others gasp and step back. The ground shakes a little, but I take a long, slow breath and urge the water beneath to be still. Then, in honour of Kayan, I form three pointed blades of ice, spin around, and throw them at the bottom step below the trapdoor.

They are so sharp, they pierce the wood, and make a thwack, thwack sound as they make contact.

There is a moment where no one speaks, and then Briony starts to clap. Yarrow joins in. So do the others. "Do you know what this means?" Yarrow asks, clapping Finn on the shoulder.

"It means this time tomorrow, we'll be free." Finn grins back at him, and they fall into a brotherly embrace. When he turns back to me, he says, "It's now or never, Alana. We have to take this chance while we have it. Before Eldrion realises you have magic."

I walk slowly over to the steps and tug on one of the shards. I pull it free and turn it over in my hand, watching the ice start to melt when it makes contact with my skin. Turning back, I fold my arms in front of my stomach. "All right. I'm in – on one condition."

"Anything," Finn says quickly.

"We break the Leafborne out of the dungeons and bring them with us."

Frowning, Yarrow opens his mouth to object, but Finn cuts him off. "Of course," he says. "I wouldn't have it any other way."

"All right, then tell me what you need me to do."

"THERE IS NO MAP OF THE TUNNELS," FINN SAYS. "WE never created one because we didn't want it to be found or used against us." He taps his head playfully. In the dim light, shadows fall on his scarred cheek and make it look smoother. Gentler.

One day, I will ask him who gave him that scar. But I think I already know the answer.

"So, you'll have to stick with Briony. *Do not* get separated."

I nod, and slip my hand into Briony's. She nods at me and nudges my shoulder with hers.

"We'll do it tomorrow night. There's to be a feast. I'll perform." Finn is thinking on his feet, speaking as the thoughts form in his head. "I have a little disappearing act I've been working on." He grins at me, his eyes twinkling. "They'll think it's part of the act, and it'll take them a while to realise what's happening." He nods at Yarrow. "You'll be on guard tomorrow night. Bring those you can trust. When they start to grow restless, tell them to be patient. Then, slip away and lock them inside the Grand Hall and *run*."

"You'll come here, and I'll go to the dungeons to free the Leafborne."

"I'll make sure everyone knows that when the drums start, they should make their way to the tunnels." A blond woman standing behind Yarrow nods firmly.

"What about Briony and me? We'll be in the Grand Hall, too?"

Finn shakes his head and bites his lower lip. "No," he says, ruminating as he starts to pace up and down. "No, you'll go to Eldrion early. You've done that before. And after what he told you tonight, he'll expect you to want to talk to him."

I exhale slowly and brush down my skirt.

"Distract him. Keep him talking as long as you can. When the Sunborne are safely locked in the Hall, Briony will come to tell Eldrion. He'll rush down there and let them out. There will be chaos for a while – I'll be sure to leave a few *tricks* to keep the show going. Then We'll meet in the dungeons. We won't have much time. But there is a tunnel entrance there, too. Hidden at the back of the dungeons.

Yarrow will make sure the guard on duty is one of ours."
Finn turns to Briony. "Take the west exit."

She frowns a moment, then says, "All right. West."

"But Alana, this is the important part." Finn turns to me.
"You're our only chance of fighting back. We have
weapons we've fashioned, and we can fight with our bare
hands. But compared to Eldrion and the rest of the
Sunborne, we're weak. If we're followed – *when* we're
followed. We will need you."

The significance of his words solidifies in my stomach.
"Not just your water affinity. Your empathy, too. You can
take people's feelings away, remember? That means you
can take their courage, their bravery, their loyalty."

My head is swimming. I start to breathe heavily and bend
over to brace my hands on my knees. Finn puts his hand
on my back.

"What is it? Alana? Are you sick?"

Shaking, I look up at him. "It all rests on my shoulders." I
run my hand up his arm and rest it on his elbow. "You've
been planning this for two entire decades, and it is all
dependent on me."

"No." Finn lowers his voice. "No, don't look at it like that.
You've given us hope, Alana. And that's what we've been
waiting for. A glimmer of hope that would spur us to do
what we need to do to be free." He pulls me into his chest
and holds me close. "I can never thank you enough for
what you're about to do for us."

Chapter Thirty-Three

ALANA

*T*HE NEXT DAY

ELDRION'S USUALLY SMOOTH HAIR IS TOUSLED, AND HE looks as though he hasn't slept. His whisky bottle is empty, and he's sitting slumped in an armchair cradling a glass with just a thimbleful of liquid remaining inside.

He doesn't even look up when I enter, just swills the last dregs of his drink around in his glass, then drinks it in one small sip.

Standing, he rubs his temples. He looks pained, but I have no idea why, and I'm not going to ask.

Finally, after I have stood in silence by the door for what feels like an eternity, waiting for him to speak, he says, "Did you ask him?"

I don't pretend to be unsure of what he's asking, just reply, "I did."

"And?" Eldrion rubs his temples again and winces. Looking past me, he casts his gaze towards the bookcase at the back of the room. Then taps his fingernails on his glass. "And . . .?" he repeats.

"He admitted you were telling the truth."

"Good. Then finally we can talk honestly with each other." Eldrion's words slur a little. He is drunk, which is proved by the fact he has to brace himself on the arm of the chair as he stands.

"Honesty? At last." I walk over to him, purposefully standing closer than I normally would. "I'd like some honesty. So, why don't you tell me why the fuck you brought me here? What is all this about? What do you *want* from me? Is it all part of some weird obsession? A crush?" I laugh, trying to find the buttons I can press to supercharge his frustration and draw him into an argument.

Eldrion simply looks me up and down, rubs his palm over his face, and laughs. "A crush?" he mutters. "You think I'd go through all this for a crush?"

Fire flames in my belly. "Perhaps."

"You are not that special, Alana Leafborne."

"Except, I am, aren't I?" I square up to him.

He looks down at me, my frame small and lithe compared to his broadness. A laugh shakes his shoulders. He looks at my hands. "You no longer wear your gloves."

"They're not necessary. You know that."

He nods slowly. "I do know."

He turns away, but I grab hold of his upper arm and force him to look at me. "By the stars, Eldrion, tell me why I'm here!"

His eyes flash. Deep, blood red. A colour that sends shivers to the darkest depths of my soul and rattles free the fears that linger there. "I can't tell you," he says. "So, let me show you."

With one hand, he takes hold of my wrist. I object, but he holds on tightly. With the other, he opens his shirt. My breath hitches. "What are you doing?"

"Quiet," he barks.

Then he slams my bare fist onto his chest. Above his heart. He fixes his eyes on mine, and his wings flash the same deep shade of crimson as his eyes.

I inhale sharply. I can't breathe. I feel like I'm choking. Like the room is filling with smoke.

A bright white light appears in front of my eyes and blinds me. I try to pull away but Eldrion holds me still until . . . everything disappears. I am standing up high, looking down on the castle and the citadel. Flying, maybe.

A scream echoes in my mind. Then another. I look down. The citadel is burning. Huge, towering, infernos of heat billow up into the sky. With them, they bring clouds of dark grey smoke. It fills the air. I cough, and turn around, desperately trying to find a way to escape.

But then there is more.

The ground shakes.

A carousel of images pummels my brain.

Crumbling walls, surging seas. Ice, and fire, and ash. Screams. Leafborne dying. Sunborne dying. Wings being ripped from their owners and bursting into flame in the air. Turning to dust.

Then Finn . . . I see Finn.

I reach for him but he turns away from me.

His mask lies at my feet. I pick it up and hold it in front of me, but as I stare at it, it disintegrates into a million purple butterflies. They surge up into the air, but then they darken. They become black and foreboding.

The entire sky is full of them, undulating, pressing down on me.

Fire, and ash, and ice, and screams.

I rip my hand away from Eldrion with a a force that makes him cry out. I stumble backwards. Sweat glistens on my brow, but my skin feels deathly pale. I stumble. And then I realise Eldrion is no longer standing in front of me. He's lying on the floor.

And he is unconscious.

Chapter Thirty-Four

FINN

I wait at the side of the room, in the shadows, as I always do. The drums start beating, and the spotlight appears. Scanning the outer edges, I spot Yarrow and he offers me a fixed stare that says, *We're ready. Now or never.*

Now. It has to be now.

I breathe in slowly and allow the vibration of the drums to settle beneath my skin.

Then I stride into the light.

As usual, the wave of energy coming from the Sunborne fae makes me nauseous. I hate them with so much passion, I still don't understand how I've lived in such close proximity to them for so long.

I open my arms and, just as planned, the ropes descend from the ceiling. Grabbing hold of them, I leverage myself up into the air and begin to perform the body-twisting dips, and dives, and spectacles they anticipate.

Each night, I vary the moves. I have to, so they don't get bored. So that Eldrion doesn't stop using me. Needing me.

But no more. From tonight, everything will be different. And soon, Eldrion will know what it means to be afraid.

Grabbing hold of the bar that is permanently suspended from the ceiling, I hook my legs over it, then dangle upside down above the crowd. I grin at them, and wave, and they point up at me. Then I reach behind my head, and unfasten my mask. With one swift movement, I let it drop.

As it falls, the piercings on my wings chime.

It lands with a thud and the crowd goes quiet.

The drums stop.

I swing back and forth, watching them. And then, with a flourish, I leverage myself up into the air . . . and disappear.

At least, that's what it looks like to them.

Clinging onto the beam in the darkness at the top of the hall, I look down at them and watch them. They stare, waiting for me to drop back down. When I don't, they start to mutter amongst themselves.

When the chatter becomes louder still, Yarrow makes his move. He silently exits his post, closing and bolting the door behind him. As he works, I swing myself onto the top of the beam, then run along the top of it towards an open window.

Outside, I cling to the side of the castle, nestling my fingers between the stones. I creep along the edge of the building, back inside at the next window, then drop down just as Yarrow and the other guards from the hall gather.

"All right." I slap his shoulder. "Let's go."

He beams at me from beneath his large beard. "Indeed," he says. "It is beyond time, my friend."

We hurry away from the hall as quickly as we can without making ourselves known. When we reach the kitchen, those who know what tonight is filter away from their posts and follow us to the trapdoor at the back of the pantry. Taking hold of the trapdoor, Yarrow raises his eyebrows at me. "What about the dungeon?" he asks.

"The dungeon?"

"The Leafborne? You promised . . ." He never wanted to free them, and doesn't care either way, but he is a good friend. And would support me if that's what I chose.

"We owe them nothing." I meet his eyes stoically. "Alana will play her part. She'll understand."

Yarrow hesitates, then flexes his fingers on his wooden axe, and nods. "Very well."

We swing ourselves down and immediately make our way through the first set of tunnels. When we arrive at the weaponry, we take what we can carry.

"Where are we exiting?" he asks. "Which tunnels?"

"East."

"You told Briony west?"

"It makes sense for us to all use different exits. No sense in us all being compromised if one tunnel is captured."

Yarrow nods, satisfied. Then he inhales deeply, flexes his shoulders, and says, "Then let's go, my friend. Let us leave this hellish place and never, ever return."

Chapter Thirty-Five

ALANA

*B*riony is waiting for me outside. I must look as shocked as I feel, because she takes one glance at me and grabs my hands. "Alana, what happened?"

I can't speak, just shake my head at her and start running in the direction of the dungeons.

When we reach them, Briony taps on the door. She is holding her breath, but releases it when she sees the guard who answers.

"Roan," she says. "Yarrow told you?"

"Yes, he told me." Roan ushers us inside. "Let's hurry."

As the fae in the cells begin to stir, Roan rushes to the door and unbolts it. "What's happening?" snaps Maura, dragging herself to her feet.

I run over and grab the bars. "It's happening. We're getting you out."

I expect there to be a flurry of movement, but no one moves an inch. They just stare at me.

Yanking open the door, Roan steps inside and begins unlocking the chains from around everyone's necks. When he reaches Maura, she flinches.

"We have to hurry." I gesture for them to start filing out, but they seem too stunned. It is Raine who speaks up.

"I don't want to die," she says, resting her hand on her belly. "I have too much to live for, Alana. I'm not risking it."

The air is practically trembling with fear. I can feel it even with my gates up. So, I do the only thing I can think of . . . Perhaps it's wrong. Perhaps it's breaking some kind of unwritten rule or breaking a barrier that shouldn't be broken. But I can't afford to stop and think about it. There isn't time.

I close my eyes and lower the gates in my mind. Immediately, their fear crashes over me like a tidal wave, threatening to pull me under. But instead of crumbling, I let it wash through me, absorbing it into my very being.

Then, just as I did before, I reach out with my powers, imagining their fear as a tangible thing, a dark, heavy mass that I can grab hold of and pull away. I focus on each person in turn, visualising their fear as a separate entity, and with a deep breath, I begin to draw it out of them.

It's not like before, when I took away their pain. This is different, more intense, more personal. I feel like I'm reaching into their very souls, touching something sacred and private. But I don't stop. I can't stop. Not now.

As I work, I feel the atmosphere in the room begin to shift. The air grows lighter, the tension easing. I open my eyes and see the fae starting to stir, their expressions changing from terror to confusion to tentative hope.

"What did you do?" whispers Briony, her eyes wide.

"I took away their fear," I reply, my voice shaking slightly. "I had to. It was the only way."

I wobble a little, but Briony catches me and wraps her arm around my waist until I am steady.

Maura steps forward, her gaze locked on mine. "You shouldn't have done that," she says, but there's no anger in her voice, only a sort of resigned understanding. "But thank you."

I nod, swallowing hard. "We have to go. Now."

This time, there's no hesitation. The fae move quickly and, as they finally start to file out of the cells, I turn to Briony. "Shouldn't Finn be here? He said he was going to meet me here . . ."

Briony looks towards the locked door. Roan rushes to the corner of the dark, cavernous space that Eldrion uses as his dungeon. He starts to move things aside. I step sideways so I can see what he's doing. They look like empty sacks. He's tossing them behind him, forming another pile, then he says, "Can someone help? I need to move him."

Pen steps forward. "What do you need?" But then his eyes widen and a wave of nausea washes over him. I slam my gates up, but too late. It washes over me too, and I clutch my throat as I bite it back down.

"We need to move him." Roan looks up. He's holding onto a pair of ankles. Rawk's ankles.

"Rawk . . ." I knew he was dead. But seeing him. Like this . . . Grey, and sunken, and rotting from the inside out . . . I turn away and clench my fist, bringing it to my mouth to try to hold in the vomit swirling in my gut.

"There's no time for squeamishness. We have to move him. Now," Roan barks.

Visibly trying not to faint, Pen takes hold of Rawk's arms and helps Roan drag him out of the way. Beneath him lies a thick piece of cloth, which Roan moves to one side to reveal a trapdoor. Just like the one in the kitchen.

Roan pulls it open. "This is it," he says. Then he looks at Briony. "Finn is certain tonight is the night?"

"You saw what she did." Briony nods in my direction. "We won't have a better chance to be free, Roan."

With a firm nod, Roan stands back. "Then, let's go," he says.

Pen goes first, then Raine. He helps her down onto the ladder and I hear him keeping check on her the entire way down. When they reach the bottom, Roan throws a box of matches down and tells them to find the lanterns. "Get them lit," he calls.

Standing aside with Maura, Briony, and me, he allows all the other Leafborne to climb down into the hatch before asking which one of us wants to go first.

"Maura . . ." I take her arm.

She flinches involuntarily, then meets my eyes and sighs.

"This is you?" she says. "You did this. You're getting us out?"

"Not just me. There's more . . ." I stop because Roan is shaking his head at me.

"Not now," he says. "There really isn't time, Alana."

I squeeze Maura's forearm. "Later, we'll talk later. But for now . . . we have to go."

I help her down onto the ladder, then wait for Briony. Roan stands back and gestures for me to go ahead of him. I hesitate, then say, "Thank you," and clamber down.

When I reach the bottom, Roan isn't far behind. The lamps are lit, and we are gathered in the damp silence of the tunnels. Explaining quickly, I tell the others that the Shadowkind are helping us escape and that Briony and Roan will be leading the way out of the citadel.

"We're really getting out?" whispers one of the young fae.

"We're really getting out," I tell her. Then I turn to Briony. She rubs her hands together and nods at me. A shudder runs through her entire body.

"Do you need me to take away your fears, too?" I ask her quietly. "This is a big moment. I can make it easier for you."

But Briony simply smiles at me. "I have waited too long for this," she says. "I want to feel every last bit of it. Good and bad."

I take her hands and grasp them tightly. "All right, then just know this . . . I am grateful for you, Briony. It has been a long time since I've had a true friend. And I know I wouldn't have survived the last few weeks without you."

For a moment, I think Briony's going to say something. Her mouth opens, then closes. She inhales deeply. But then she steels herself and says, "All right. No more talk. It's time. This way."

As we start to move through the tunnels, the weight of what we're doing settles in the crevices between my muscles and makes my body ache. The air is heavy with the scent of damp earth, and the sound of our footsteps echoes off the walls. The Leafborne huddle close together, their faces a mix of fear and hope.

Roan and Briony lead the way, their steps sure and steady. They've been planning this for so long. Two hundred years. I cannot even imagine the weight of what this means to *them*.

We walk for what feels like hours, the tunnels twisting and turning, taking us deeper and deeper beneath the citadel. With each step, I anticipate hearing the thunder of guards behind us. But there is nothing. Just silence.

As we round another corner, however, Pen holds up a hand, signalling for us to stop. He tilts his head, listening intently. "Do you hear that?" he whispers.

I strain my ears, trying to pick out any sound over the pounding of my own heart. At first, there's nothing. But then, faint and distant, I hear it. The sound I dreaded . . .

"Alana Leafborne . . ." My name drifts on a breeze that whips through the tunnels. "You cannot escape me."

"He's coming," Roan says, his voice tight with tension. "Eldrion knows we're gone."

A ripple of fear passes through the group, and I feel it like a physical thing, pressing down on my chest. I want to reach out, to take it away from them again, but I'm so tired. I don't know if I have the strength.

"What do we do?" Raine asks, moving closer to Pen.

Roan and Briony exchange a glance. "We keep moving," Briony says finally. "We're close to the exit. If we can just make it a little farther . . ."

She doesn't finish the sentence, but she doesn't need to. We all know what's at stake. If Eldrion catches us now, there will be no mercy. No second chances.

"Alana Leafborne!" Eldrion is closer now, and his voice brings the images back. The ones I was trying to forget.

"GO!" I yell for Briony and Roan to keep running. "Don't stop. I'll catch up. It's me he wants, and I'm the only one with magic."

"You won't find the way," Briony yells.

"They all exit somewhere, right?"

Briony hesitates, then nods.

"Then I'll find you. Now, go!"

Chapter Thirty-Six

ELDRION

My entire body throbs with a mixture of pain and power. It is a surge I haven't felt for centuries, since my own powers started to grow and transition into their fullest form.

Something new is inside me.

And I know it came from her.

Clambering onto my knees, I grip hold of the armchair and pull myself up to my feet. My body feels heavy with the weight of its new knowledge.

The knowledge that she is *everything* I ever needed. But she could be everything that will destroy me.

Because she saw what I saw. I know deep in my soul that she saw the flames, and heard the screams, and watched Luminael crumbling. But I still do not know if she is its saviour or its damnation.

All I know is I have to find her.

I am at the door when it is flung open. A guard with a red, sweat-laced complexion braces his hands on the frame and pants loudly.

"What happened?" I bark.

He meets my eyes. "My lord. The jester. He has disappeared, and many of the servants, too. It seems . . ." He hesitates. "It seems they are trying to escape, my lord."

A surge of rage courses through my veins, hot and fierce. My wings flare out behind me, filling the room with their shadow. The guard takes a step back.

"The Leafborne prisoners," I growl, my voice low and dangerous. "What of them?"

The guard swallows hard, his Adam's apple bobbing in his throat. "They're gone, my lord. The cells are empty."

A roar of fury tears from my throat, and I lash out, my fist connecting with the stone wall. Pain lances through my knuckles, but I barely feel it. All I can feel is the white-hot anger consuming me, the overwhelming need to find her, to bring her back.

She has seen what I have seen, felt what I have felt. And now, she is running from me, taking with her my only hope of understanding what it means.

I cannot let that happen.

I will not let that happen.

I stride to the window, my gaze sweeping over the citadel below. I will find her. I will bring her back. And I will make her understand that she belongs to me, that her destiny is intertwined with mine in ways neither of us can comprehend.

"My lord?" the guard stutters.

I turn around, and stride towards him. "Who else is missing?"

The guard's eyes widen.

"The jester? Where is he?"

Again, the guard's mouth opens and closes. "We do not know, my lord. He disappeared in the middle of his act. The doors were locked. Your guests were —"

I look him up and down. His face is familiar. It is weak, and pathetic, and useless to me. I take my dagger from my belt and thrust it into his side.

He wavers, falls, and slumps against the door. I kick him away, step over him, then fly for the dungeons.

Chapter Thirty-Seven

ALANA

*D*eep in the tunnels, back towards the dungeons, a thunderous roar shakes the soil above and below us. The tunnels are small, built this way on purpose because Eldrion is so large, and yet he is following us anyway.

Briony is still lingering when Roan grabs her arm. "Henrik told me to take care of you if anything ever happened to him, so that's what I'm going to do." Then in one swift movement, he hoists her onto his shoulder and runs.

I wait a moment, trying to catch my breath, and then, deliberately, I choose the tunnel beside the one Briony took. In its entrance, I stop, rip a piece of my skirt and leave it lying on the ground. Then I run. He will catch up with me, but I run anyway. I run until I can feel the weight of the low tide pressing down upon the top of the tunnels. Then stop, and wait.

When he appears, his entire body is taut, tense, coiled, ready to unleash his fury on me.

All this time, I have wondered what his magic looks like. What it is that makes him so very powerful. It seems I'm finally about to find out.

"Wait." His voice surprises me. It lands like hot oil on my skin and makes me flinch. "What did you see?" he asks.

His face is cast in shadow, making his ice-blue eyes shine even brighter in the darkness. I shake my head and flex my fingers at my sides. "You know what I saw. You *made* me see it. That's what you do, isn't it? Cast visions? Make people see things that aren't there?"

Eldrion's expression is unreadable. I search his body, his mind, his soul. But all that comes back to me is a blank-ness. A misty, dark, blankness. It fizzes like static and fills my mind with pinpricks of pain. Why can't I read him? Is he blocking me? All this time, he's been able to block me?

He tilts his head, studying my face, and then he sighs heav-ily. "I do not cast visions, Alana. I receive visions." He steps closer. I want to move away, but my body won't cooperate. He towers over me. He could extinguish me right now, in a heartbeat, if he wanted to. The way he extinguished Kayan.

As a surge of rage rushes to my throat, I realise what I have to do.

I have to keep him here as long as it takes for the others to escape. Because if they are free, at least Kayan's death won't have been in vain.

"You *receive* visions?" I scoff. "Like a prophet?"

Eldrion's features remain set into a stony glare. "Like a seer," he growls. "I am a seer, Alana. And what you saw was not some conjuring. It was real. All of it."

Again, the images flood my brain. Fire, ice, crumbling walls, blood, and fury, and death, and . . .

"Us," I breathe.

"What did you say?" Eldrion is so close to me now that I can almost feel his heart beating beneath his skin. Shirtless, his wings tucked into the cramped space of the tunnel, frame filling the entire space, he glistens with sweat. He takes my chin in his hand. "What did you say, Alana?"

I stare up at him, and my voices comes out as a breathy whisper. "I saw you. You were watching a vision of us. Me and you. We were . . ." I trail off. Something is happening to my body. Anger, guilt and shame are met by treacherous, swirling, ropes of lust that tie my organs in knots as I look at him. "We were fucking, and you were touching yourself. You came while you watched us come. I thought it was make-believe. A fantasy." I am breathing faster. My skin fizzes with tension.

Eldrion's eyes skim my features, linger on my lips, then drop down to the swell of my breasts. The cords of muscle in his naked shoulders twitch. "It was not a fantasy," he breathes. And then he grabs hold of me. One hand on my waist, the other at my throat, he slams me back against the inner wall of the tunnel. I grab his fingers. He loosens his grip, moving his hand to snake up into my hair.

And then his lips crash onto mine.

He kisses me with the force of a gale or a thunderstorm. Engulfing my entire body with the power of his passion. His tongue meets mine. His hands roam my body.

Feverishly, I pull my dress up as he tugs my underwear to the side. I bite his lower lip, drawing blood, and he jerks my head back roughly, glowering at me. I meet his eyes defiantly and watch as he slowly licks the blood from his lip, gives my hair another tug, then kisses me again. Softer this time. Searching.

As he enters me, he pulls my dress down and devours my breasts with his mouth. I grab the back of his head and hold his lips on my nipple as he swirls, and sucks, and bites.

He thrusts harder, groans my name, and the sound it makes drives me into oblivion.

This time, it's not visions of fire and ash and ice that blind me. It is visions of sweat, and skin. Red flesh, chains, pain that turns into pleasure. Eldrion holds my hands above my head. My wings flutter, keeping me upright while he comes inside me, then – holy stars – curls the tip of his wing around my body and uses it to push me over the edge of my orgasm.

I climax in waves, silently screaming as my muscles freeze, harden, then slowly melt around him.

He pants into my neck. His body is shaking.

"Did you see this?" I ask, pulling back, staring at him.

He stares back at me. Still inside me, he growls, "No, I did not."

With a gentle push, I make him back away. I'm surprised when he obeys the gesture, pulling his pants up and watching me rearrange my dress.

"Alana . . ."

I shake my head. My cheeks are flushed, my hair loose, my entire body alive with something that feels both so wrong and so right at the same time. But I know what I have to do.

Slowly, I back away from him. "That shouldn't have happened," I mutter. "I love Finn."

"The jester is not all you think he is, Alana. Come back with me. I will show you."

"Why should I trust you?" I scrape my fingers through my hair. "I cannot trust you."

Rage simmers in Eldrion's eyes, but I do not see it replicated in his aura. Still, all I see is a mist. A haziness I cannot catch hold of.

I flex my fingers at my sides. He hasn't noticed. He's just staring at me. His hand goes to his belt, where he holds a knife. The knife he used to slit Kayan's throat.

"Tell me where you buried Kayan's body." The words come suddenly and unexpectedly. Perhaps I'm giving him one last chance to show me there's a glimmer of anything other than pure villainy nestled beneath his skin.

"I can't."

"Why?"

"I can't tell you."

I tilt my head up, bite my lower lip. "Then fuck you, my lord." With a roar, I splay my fingers and jump back. The tunnel starts to shake. I close my eyes. I feel the water that lives above us, the damp of the sand at low tide that surrounds the citadel. I call to it. I think of Kayan, and picture his body falling, and I hear his scream.

It builds inside me, grows, and grows, and claws against my insides because it is desperate to be free.

And with it, his magic grows, too.

I feel it so strongly that when I open my eyes, I am floating above the ground – and my wings are no longer just purple. They are flecked with blue.

The light casts an eerie glow on the walls of the tunnel. Eldrion watches them, transfixed, then seems to realise what is happening and attempts to rush towards me.

I pull my arms in towards my body with a yell. The walls split, and water sweeps Eldrion from his feet. He beats his wings, but can't right himself. I stay above it all, watching. Then I let Kayan's scream break free from my chest.

The walls of the tunnel collapse. The ceiling collapses. Water and earth pile down on top of Eldrion and the last thing I hear as I turn and flee is his muffled cries.

As I move, the tunnels continue to collapse behind me. I keep flying, keep flying, until the ground is dry and I'm able to lower myself to my feet. As my bare soles touch the damp earth, I brace my hands on the sides of the tunnel and try to find my breath.

After several long minutes, standing, shaking, still feeling the wetness between my legs from where he fucked me, I drag myself forward. I walk for what feels like hours, but could only be minutes, until I see light up ahead.

Muted daylight.

When I reach it, I look up. It is filtering down through a nest of twigs and leaves. Next to me is a ladder made of rope.

I grab hold of it and climb.

Pre-Order

Continue The Story - Pre-Order out June 25th 2024 **HERE**

Join Alexis On REAM

Get exclusive access to stories before they are released on REAM STORIES.

Made in the USA
Middletown, DE
27 November 2024

65525934R00156